For my darling wife,
and my beautiful children
William & Edward

A huge thank you to Steph
and Andrea for all your hard work

Hidden

Chapter 1
The Hitman

Teatro La Fenice, Venice

The assembled orchestra was playing Palladio 1: Allegretto by Karl Jenkins. Each chord was melodic and every note reverberated tunefully. The very essence of the prosody embodied the elegance and history, character and beauty of the ancient theatre. The audience was enraptured, taken by the masterful strings.

"Too modern for my palate." Snapped an indignant old Italian man down his large nose from the first tier box above the stalls. His twenty years junior pocket-sized, trophy wife's swollen and puckered rigid botoxed lips smiling stupidly in agreement. Several guests congregated around him nodded sheepishly in unison. Others scowled in disgust at his harsh comment.

Massimo just laughed at them all. Their pretensions and aristocratic ignorance amused him more than anything. He stood up brushing the elegant silk lapels of his tailored tuxedo. He rather enjoyed the fabric's simple softness on his rough hands, one of his idiosyncrasies.

With a nod to the beautiful young woman sitting next to him he excused himself making for the rear of the crowded theatre. Stepping out from the gloom of the dimly lit atmospheric box office the Italian midday summer sun radiated above him. 'Ah, Venice…' he smiled as two sensational Italian ladies graced past him with a lustful stare at his young charm, handsome looks and visible athleticism. He slipped his Bang and Olufsen Beoplay Specialised earbuds in and tapped his watch as Muse's Supermassive Black Hole's iconic guitar riff boomed in high definition within his ears. He exhaled heavily, closing his cold eyes. 'Play time…' he smiled as he made his way across the Ponte Maria Callas that bridged the rio della Vesta.

The ancient weathered labyrinthine walls along the Calle Del Piovan O Gritti were littered with the exposed skeleton of gnarled thin red bricks amid the crumbling plaster dotted with obnoxious graffiti of the idle local youth and idiotic tourists leaving their mark on the historic buildings. The walls now only a mere shadow of the once grand buildings of Venice. He had chosen the route knowing it to be a quieter area from tourism, vaporetto and boat traffic, the Canale della Galeazze snaked around several beautiful locations, the Santa Maria del Giglio and the Gran Teatro La Fenice where he had just left.

The narrow path fed through to the Palazzo Marin, he stopped lowering his head and turning subtly around firstly to allow a small group of tourists to file past, their cameras, mobiles and selfie sticks poised and ready as they captured every inch of the Venetian backstreet. And secondly to ensure his face wouldn't appear on any of their images. He only lifted his head once all had moved along. Checking the dial on his Digital Breitling he pressed on determinedly through the narrow streets.

He walked into the sixteenth century palace amid a throng of people dressed in ball gowns and tuxedos. The low-ceilinged corridor of the Palazzo Marin was dimly lit by eight large iron lanterns that cast the guests' shadows all along the walls. He climbed the first set of marble stairs up to a beautifully decorated room adorned with masterpieces and furniture from the past three hundred years. A grand piano in the corner was accompanied by a string quartet all dressed in Georgian wigs and tails. Massimo quickly scanned the room, the chandeliers illuminating what he estimated to have been sixty guests had already arrived. 'Not here.' He said to himself as he continued through the palace. He continued through the magnificent building, his sharp eyes taking in every detail of the décor, the neo classical busts, the eighteenth-century frescoes of The flight of Helen from Troia, Theseus and Ariadne among so many others. He entered a formal room where a large tapestry hung from one of the walls, it was illuminated by five small spotlights that hung from metal arms from the ceiling. Along the next wall stood a huge wooden cabinet with a large door leading off either side. The door on the left was where he wanted to go. Massimo looked around at the mixture of more modern 19th and 20th century art that adorned the walls, he thought it odd how each wall contradicted the other. But then he stopped himself. Across the candle lit room he saw the man he had come to see. His target.

Massimo removed his earbuds and pocketed them, taking a glass of Champagne from a costumed waiter and moved closer to the nearest wall for cover. Not ten feet from him stood two men guarding the very door he needed to enter, these men looked fierce, large and hairy.

They resembled the Italian Rugby Union star Martín Leandro Castrogiovanni and wore matching black pin-stripe Armani suits that swelled around their colossal arms and barrelled chest. Tailored and sleek but leaving little to the imagination. Between their hairy heads Massimo caught the target's face once more as he socialised with other guests, nonchalant and completely oblivious to what was about to unravel before them.

A final glance at his watch, he focused his mind, calmed his breath and honed in on all his senses, every sound, movement and change in the air from passing guests, his nostrils tracing their expensive perfumes and aftershaves as they brushed past him making their way along the dimly lit corridor. He finished his glass of Champagne and pressed a tiny ceramic disc to the base of the glass foot before placing it on top of an antique dresser next to him. Placing a hand into his suit pocket he pulled out and slipped on a thin black glove onto his right hand, three of the gloves fingertips and the thumb were topped with several small concentric circles where his fingerprints sat beneath.

"It is time." Massimo's inner monologue began narrating his next moves, his plan of attack in order of how he would process and subsequently remove the hostiles before him so he could reach his target in the most effective and efficient way. He had, as always planned the execution meticulously weeks before, but his experience had taught him to never underestimate his target, or the unpredictability of human behaviour.

His cold eyes flitted across the room as his mind raced through scenario after scenario until his eyes once again stopped on the target in the next room.

Three large strides forward and he stood before the two rugby players, one lazily held an extended tree trunk of an arm up to stop Massimo with little more than a shake of his head whilst the other side stepped to close the gap between them blocking Massimo's route through the ornate doorway.

Massimo smiled gently at them, then grabbed the first man's proffered wrist with his black gloved hand, within a second the rugby player appeared to convulse silently as a small spittle of foam began protruding from the side of his mouth. Massimo released his grip of the man's wrist and slapped the glove onto rugby player two's solid chest, exactly as the first man had; he began convulsing violently as foam emitted from his nose and mouth. The men remained standing and as still as sentinel statues whilst Massimo walked effortlessly between them. From within the room everything appeared normal, the two security guards were still standing sentry at their post as they should be. Little did the people inside the small room know they were both now actually dead.

Keeping his head down Massimo moved like a shadow through the candle lit room until he stood directly behind his target. His left hand felt for the fob in his trouser pocket, then he pressed it. Outside the room his champagne glass exploded at the base with a small pop sending the shattered glass outwards in a small shimmering cloud onto the polished floor. Everyone in the room looked up at the unexpected disturbance, everyone except Massimo. With the room distracted he placed his gloved right hand on his target's temple. The unknown man silently gritting his teeth as his entire body began cavorting.
Three seconds later Massimo was exiting the room as the costumed servers rushed along the corridor to clean the fallen shattered glass.

Massimo was already back downstairs before he heard the first scream, then another, and another. Walking swiftly he made it out to the foyer where gondola drivers sat in wait for their clients to return after the party. No one even looked up at him as they sat chatting and smoking. He turned a corner and was about to leave the compound when a young man with an earpiece stopped him.

'Fermati lì.' snapped the young man holding up a palm. Massimo looked at him, his Italian was good but the accent wasn't Italian, Swiss maybe. That meant one of two things, mercenary... Or, Vatican Swiss Guard.

The young man spoke into his sleeve cuff as he looked Massimo up and down. Then he moved closer to him looking over his shoulder to the gondola drivers, *"Stupid move."* thought Massimo to himself. The young man then clawed hopelessly at Massimo's arm as it wrapped around in a vice-like grip around the man's neck. He left the dead body where it lay, no point in dropping it in the water, it would just float and be more obvious. Besides, Polizia would be all over the palace in a matter of minutes. Why make more work for himself?

He swiftly made his way back across the Ponte Maria Callas until he was back outside the theatre when his mobile phone began to ring.
'Si. E 'fatto. It is done... Not now, transfer it to the Singapore account.' he spat as he tried to keep his voice lower than a whisper. 'I have a concert to finish and a Bulgarian supermodel to pleasure. Si, domani.' He cleared the line, pocketing his phone.

He tapped his watch with a broad grin, 'All done in under five minutes.' he chuckled to himself as he returned to the cool gloomy belly of the theatre. Sitting down he passed his beautiful Bulgarian date another glass of champagne. The orchestra struck up another brilliant rendition of Franz Joseph Haydn's Symphony No.104 in D Major led by Dmitry Matvienko. His date's petite hand squeezed and brushed his muscular thigh before moving up towards his crotch. Massimo raised an eyebrow and smiled as he sipped his champagne.

*

Massimo woke with a broad smile as he opened his dark eyes taking in the naked shoulder, exposed rib cage and waist of the beautiful Bulgarian lady that lay silently sleeping beside him. He kissed her soft shoulder gently then rolled himself out of the king size bed without so much as rustle from the silk bed sheets. He showered and shaved before dressing in a light tailored blue shirt and comfortable chino trousers. His sunglasses placed delicately on his styled thick wavy head of hair he smiled at his reflection in the antique gold gilt framed mirror that hung in the hotel suite's hallway. The sun was bright as he exited the Baglioni Hotel Luna, another hot summer's day as he passed the already rampant tourists and made his way around the corner into St. Mark's square.

He took a seat at a small café and ordered himself an espresso. He smoked a cigarette and watched the world pass him by whilst he waited for his drink. He didn't have to wait long before his small white porcelain cup and saucer were delivered by a cute long haired waitress.

His strong fingers gripped the miniature handle as he swigged down the rich hot black liquid. His phone buzzed on the table as he picked it up looking at the number, he exhaled the smoke of his cigarette before answering.

'Pronto?' he asked inquisitively.

'Signor Lupo, we must commend you on your last work... A true masterpiece.' came the suspect male voice. It was European but had been through a filter and pitch distortion app making it untraceable. For all he knew he could be on the phone to a Jamaican lady.

'Grazie mille.' He replied emptily. He watched with a scrutinising frown as he observed the young couple sitting beside him. Tourists, Spanish, students, early twenties, upper class but loved to believe they were bohemian. *"I bet they smoke weed and read Carl Marx books at college"* he thought to himself. Both enjoying their cappuccino coffee, croissant and Jam. He sucked his teeth indignantly and returned to the call.

'An opportunity has arisen that we would like you to apply for.' came the voice. He never understood why they always talked in riddles and codes, everybody knew that the world governments monitored mobile phone calls for trigger words and suspect activity.

It was the inevitable bastard child of 1950's J. Edgar Hoover paranoia hysteria *"we are always listening"* but nowadays technology has all gone digital. But little did people realise that with the birth of social media, everyone spoke their mind, regardless of the consequences meaning that the government now had to monitor 3 billion accounts on multiple formats. This meant that nobody was interested in Massimo's clandestine telephone call with his mysterious patreon.

'Where?' he spoke as he nodded, checking his watch, 'I can be in London by 1700hrs.'

'Name?' he enquired.

'All details will be sent through to your handler as per usual.' replied the distorted voice.

'Va bene, it will be done.' continued Massimo as he concluded the conversation.

He had always been told not to ask questions, not to get involved, not to ask why. But in his own mind he had always tried to piece together the motive or agenda behind each hit. The majority of his work was politically motivated, one person wanted to take out their opposition. But the last few months had been different, felt different. Something deep within him had begun to notice a pattern. A convoluted link between his targets. Most of whom had come from this mysterious patron.

For the first time in his long career Massimo had started to question himself.

*

Chapter 2
The Secret

British Museum, London

The opaque moss covered skylight tapped incessantly from the irregular unseasonal summer downpour. The morose ominous grey skies above London continued to unleash the bulbous droplets.

Sat directly below, deep within the dimly lit *"Restricted Access Area"* of the British Museum Library and Archive, Genevieve Silankis slipped on her soft white cotton conservation gloves to turn the page of the delicate Lindisfarne Gospel manuscript that lay open before her atop its rare book display pillow. Her dark eyes lit up with excitement as they took in the full wonder of the beautifully detailed illustration surrounding the giant initial letter at the top of the ancient manuscript. She held back a cheer of delight as her gloved fingers found the small open eye symbol hidden within the gold leaf illumination, biting her lip in a mixture of both anticipation and apprehension at what she believed to be hidden beneath the gold leaf illumination.
'Could it really be-' she muttered to herself in an almost whisper.

She paused in trepidation as she centred her dizzying attention to the impressive detailed decoration of the early manuscript. Like all tomes of the eighth and ninth century their magnificence had understandably always been revered and praised due not only to the craftsmanship and unparalleled skill but the physical man hours it took to produce, each page could take a solitary or even a team of Monks anything between a week and several months to complete.

Genevieve had worked on hundreds of historical manuscripts, tomes and ledgers for her MA in History and Archaeology, and again later when working on her PhD in Ancient History. She had spent years tucked away in libraries, museums and private collections hidden from public view enhancing her interdisciplinary study. Her career in identifying and attaining lost mediaeval reliquaries and relics, antiquities and historical items got her a position at the Oxford centre for the study of religious relics at Keble College's Advanced Studies Centre (ASC). She later worked freelance for the British Museum Research Repository where she got paid to travel the world searching for lost relics.

Her latest engagement had led her back to the British Museum rare books and manuscripts room. Home to over 300,000 volumes dedicated to the research of human culture. A room reserved for only the most senior collections officers.

She brushed her hair back and sneaked a look over her shoulder to the portly security guard standing sentinel behind her. His gaze lost in oblivion against the opposite pale green wall. He appeared to be asleep with his eyes open. She turned back to the ancient calfskin vellum book and held her hands reverently just off and above the page, admiring the beautifully painted gold letters.

She recalled a documentary on the arduous processes and dedication of the Monks who'd painstakingly detailed these masterpieces by no more than candlelight, as she mimicked a squint in the dimly lit room.
This action began a chain reaction of thought process as she suddenly recalled how the famous diarist Samuel Pepys had written that he'd gone blind from excessive work by candlelight during the winter.

A Glaswegian Anthropologist friend of hers had laughed heartily at the medical myth of studying by candlelight and going blind stating, in her harsh but beautiful Scottish accent, "one would only have difficulty in *focusing* when reading in poor light, it also makes you blink less, which can lead to the eyes becoming dry and uncomfortable but never blind."

She snapped back into the room focusing all her attention on what lay before her. Biting her bottom lip, she gently scratched at the corner of the illustration just above the small open eye symbol. Like an ancient scratch card, the golden leaf foil lifted away under her gloved thumb nail. She laughed nervously, 'Flint you son of a bitch.' she shook her head in disbelief. Restraining a broad smile as beneath her now shaking hand a word appeared on the newly scratched surface. "*INTER*". 'Latin' she said to herself quietly, 'but what does it say?' She removed her mobile telephone discreetly from her tweed suit jacket, taking a series of photographs of the newly discovered word that had lain hidden for thirteen hundred years.

Genevieve swallowed hard, controlling her excited breath as she gently turned to another page of the thirteen hundred year old manuscript. She noticed several pages had been removed from the beginning of the Gospel at some point in its history. She frowned as she wondered where these severed pages now lay. She turned to another page until she found the next small open eye symbol hidden within the detailed artistry. She repeated the scratching process several times until she had discovered all the hidden words within the gospel. Noting down the words she closed the manuscript, just as the security guard coughed loudly behind her. Taking this as her cue, she took her leave from the museum.

Genevieve ran along the puddled pavements of Great Russell Street towards the Kingsway. Her destination was Waterloo Bridge over the obsidian grey surface of the Thames then along the Bankside and up through the myriad of streets to the Old Vic arts theatre. She half ran and half jogged between the umbrella toting and poncho donned tourists with her phone pressed hard to her ear. Her damp hair blowing wildly in the dreich summer wind.

'Cortez, I found it...' she exclaimed excitedly. 'Just as I thought it would be. It reads, "Between Minsters East and West lies the King's secret confessors know best". Just like the one we saw in Cambridge last year.' She slowed to a stop as a taxi rushed past her, almost knocking her elbow with its wing mirror. Checking the road was clear she dashed across the road heading into the narrow colonnaded frontage of the Old Vic.
'The letters from The Rare Book collections of Cambridge University Library detailed the open eye symbol, and it was true, every page that had this marker revealed a hidden word.'

Taking three steps at a time she moved swiftly up the open square spiral staircase. She paused outside a nondescript paint chipped wooden door that read *"Security - Authorised Personnel Only"*, she attempted to flatten her bedraggled hair with her free hand but gave up very quickly. Knocking twice she let herself in before an answer came from inside.

She slumped down into an old brown tattered and scuffed leather sofa and puffed out her reddened cheeks, hanging up her phone. She was fit and used to running but not normally dressed in a thick wet tweed suit and heavy blouse, nor did she usually run in her designer heels for that matter.

She took off her sodden jacket and threw it to her side and slipped off her wet Jimmy Cho's before opening a bottle of chilled water that had been handed to her by the large man sitting opposite her.

He sat back in his large swivel chair and grinned broadly at her. Placing a miniature remote control drone and screwdriver down on the desk he rummaged in one of his desk drawers. 'Here you go dove.' he smiled affectionately, throwing an old hand towel at her which she tosselled over her damp hair.
'You got it working yet?' she asked, looking at the pocket sized drone.
'Almost there.' he smiled.
'You know, normal people don't dismantle their birthday presents.' she retorted.
'Ha,' he chuckled lightly, 'Well, I'm not normal people.'
'Indeed you are not Cortez.' she smiled warmly back at him.

He was known to all as Cortez, but his real name was Simon Lewes. Genevieve was one of only a handful that knew his Chirsitan name. He worked as head of security at a majority of London's iconic arts and performance theatres but what earned him his moniker was his unhealthy fascination and obsession with ancient treasures, especially gold. The nickname Cortez came from this very obsession and much like the original Conquistador he too revelled in its aureate beauty. Standing an impressive six foot four, the bearded two hundred and seventy pound gentle giant's broad bear-like chest was adorned with several large and very heavy golden chains, he looked akin to a poor taste large caucasian replica of the A-Team's Mr T. He had the appearance of a grizzly powerlifting professional rugby player but was gifted with the polymath mind of an Oxford professor with a penchant for treasure hunting and computer hacking. A useful concoction of skills and attributes Genevieve had relied on many times before.

'These are amazing Genny,' he started. He knew the shortened moniker really annoyed her, but he used it anyway. 'I just cannot believe your theory worked...' he whistled loudly as he opened the photographic images she had sent to him as she had been sprinting across London. The images appeared together on a large desktop monitor beside him. 'What date is this text from?' he asked as he scrolled through the high-definition images on the large screen.

'8th century, it was created in the Holy Island Priory in Lindisfarne by the resident monks.' she replied excitedly. She paused to smell the hand towel Cortez had thrown her as her cheeks greened at the offensive smell. Tossing it to the floor she continued, 'Luckily this Gospel was taken south to Winchester in December of 792 AD for the Christmas Mass. Several months before the first Viking raiding party arrived that resulted in the destruction of the majority of the other resident gospels and texts still at Lindisfarne. One of the most significant attacks of piracy on one of England's holiest religious centres in north-western Europe.'

Cortez shook his head in awe. 'Beautiful...' he smiled to himself. His face now only inches from the large flat screen. 'So... Confessors...' he started with a raised eyebrow. 'Catholic Law? Never understood the logic of confession and how it abolishes your sins. And how some man, or woman,' he quickly added as Genevieve looked sideways at him, 'Dressed in a fancy dress robe provides criminals with absolution. Or that they do not need to disclose said crime to the proper authorities.'

Genevieve looked across to him, shaking her head. 'I think it refers to a more notable Confessor.' She looked at him with her bright smile, 'When I was back in the Museum I had a thought it could be Edward the Confessor.'

He nodded and began tapping away on his computer whilst she spoke. But then he interjected,

'But he wasn't born until much later Genny, meaning these hidden markings weren't added until much later.' commented Cortez. 'This manuscript is from the 8th century, and Edward was from the 11th century. That leaves a window of over two hundred years.'

'You're right, but it is a starting point.' replied Genevieve in agreement.

'The symbology itself is rather interesting. The open eye symbol has been used for millennia by dozens of groups, religions and organisations. The Egyptians, with their Eye of Horus and Eye of Ra, the Greeks have the Evil Eye. The Catholics used it to symbolise God watching mankind. And then there's the Illuminati with their all seeing eye.'

She hesitated as she brought up a map of London on her tablet. 'As for the East and West Minsters, that's easy enough.' she smiled typing two of London's most iconic locations into the search engine. 'East minster is St Pauls and West minster, St Peters. Edward the confessor moved the seat of power from Winchester to Westminster and built St Peters after he saw a "vision" or something like that.' She spoke to herself as she typed fervently. 'But what is the secret you are referring to?' she looked at her notes scribbled on her notebook.

Cortez spun in his ridiculously expensive ergonomic office chair as he read aloud the notes that now covered a section of his screen. 'So Westminster was an ancient passing place known as Thorny Island, it was only accessible during low tide but remained a terribly boggy marsh for hundreds of years.'

Genevieve bit her lip, her trait for when she was deep in thought or excited. 'For the Church to agree to establish and build an abbey and palace of this magnitude on the site of a bog marsh, there must have been a very good reason. It would have cost millions.' She pulled herself up and off the old pock marked sofa and came to stand beside her large friend. 'Can you bring up some old maps of London?'

'Anything in particular?' he asked as his hands typed away on his letter-worn ergonomic keyboard.

She leant over grabbing her notebook, inside was a dogeared TFL London Tube map. Opening it she showed a sketch she had drawn whilst still at the British Museum. Cortez could see from where he was the unmistakable meandering outline of the Thames beneath the labyrinthine squiggles of colourful crossing tube lines. Like a pair of lopsided John Lennon round framed glasses she had drawn two large circles with a connecting line between them scribbled on the sketch, inside these circles were two small red cruciform shapes laying east to west. 'I had a hunch you would ask.' She grinned across to him, handing over the tube map.

Cortez opened up a digital modern OS street map so that it took up half of the large flat screen monitor. Leaning closer to her he quickly scanned his eyes over the tattered tube map she had drawn on and smiled politely. Picking up his white Apple digital pencil stylus from his desk he tapped the large monitor and drew a circle and a cross onto the screen.
'St. Paul's Cathedral right.' He moved his thick hairy sausage fingers down the river to the next location and again scribbled another circle with a red cross marker inside, 'And, Westminster?'

He created a digital line between the two points as the circles converted from his oval squiggles into perfectly aligned silver aureoles with sharp red crosses in the centre. He positioned them so they lay exactly over the two highlighted minsters then sat back from the monitor and tapped the halfway point. 'Waterloo. Or thereabouts.'

"Between Minsters East and West lies the King's secret confessors know best" he repeated tapping his desk in thought. 'So what is at Waterloo?'
'Can you look for any notes from the construction of the Waterloo underground station?' she asked excitedly.

'Anomalies or ancient structures?' asked Cortez rhetorically.

'That's the general idea.' she replied, 'I am going to look into Thorney Island first, then we can look into St. Pauls.' She lowered her head and began her research. Cortez knew better than to continue talking whilst she worked beside him. He had discovered long ago that she would become lost in her trails of thought and unless the fire alarm were to sound she wouldn't hear a word he was saying.

He clicked the limescale encrusted kettle on to boil and carried on looking at his own computer, pausing only to add two tea bags to some chipped mugs before handing one to his old friend. He kept the stained mug that read "Best Boss" on the side and slurped joyfully licking the milky tea from his bushy moustache.

'Perfeck.' he grinned, perching some glasses onto the tip of his nose as he continued working.

She reviewed the scribbled notes she had taken and read them aloud. Breaking the silence. 'Thorney Island (Thorn Ait / Eyot / Ey) – An ancient ford and crossing for the Thames, its lowest or shallowest point was at the current site of Westminster, so the main north-south road almost certainly ran south-eastwards from Wheathampstead to modern Westminster. It then swung east, south of the Thames towards Canterbury, the line the Romans used as the main crossing for Watling street. St. Peter's Monastery or Westminster, was built over it in 960-1060 by Edward the Confessor.'

'Like I said,' interjected Cortez, 'If it does relate to Edward, that would leave a two hundred year window for whomever left these clues.'

She continued to read aloud from the notes on her tablet, 'Thorney is described in an 8th century charter of King Offa of Mercia as a "terrible place". In 893, Edward the Elder, son of Alfred the Great, forced invading Vikings to take refuge on Thorney Island.' She took another swig from her now lukewarm cup of tea before continuing reading, 'Over time the monks tamed the island of brambles, and by the time of Edward the Confessor it was "*A delightful place, surrounded by fertile land and green fields*".' she frowned, 'No mention of any secrets here. The only other mention is Oxford Street.'

Cortez looked at an old map of London as he said aloud, 'Before Oxford Street took its present name in the 18th century, it was known as Tyburn Road. This led to the hanging gallows at Tyburn. The Tyburn River was the second river that cut the island off from the mainland.' He pointed to the area of Westminster to the left of the map. 'Sadly there is nothing else of much interest regarding Tyburn and no mention of anything significantly Bronze Age or ritual.'

'Keep digging, we need to search for more clues. Let's go back further in time to see if we are missing anything else. Let me know what you find.' she asked her friend enthusiastically.

*

Ten minutes passed before Cortez shot his head up from his screen in excitement, 'Here we go... Got a hit on my search for ancient stones from the London & South Western Railway company... Waterloo underground station plans and architectural notes from 1846-1848...' he called over to her not looking up from his monitor.

'Mostly geological notes, looks like the whole area is a construction nightmare. This area is completely artificial and most of the modern structures are a maze of underpinning and piles, helped by the modern bankment to calm the effects of the tidal current. Blah, blah, blah.' he read in a mutter until he found what he was looking for. 'This should be the part regarding the stone...Oh, hang on, think I have found something...' he enlarged the document and scanned it quickly with his eyes, 'It states that the miners found a large monolith or standing stone within a large walled chamber that had partially collapsed, most likely to their mining and excavations. It states that the large stone and another smaller stone that they'd found further along the line were later set beneath Westminster within the new foundations during development to better support the underneath of the Houses of Parliament.' He clicked some more links but soon swore under his breath. 'The records have been redacted...' he sighed sitting back in his expensive chair making it creak under his weight. He tapped the screen at an old Victorian document that contained mostly lines of blacked out sensitive information.

Genevieve leaned in closer and sighed heavily, 'Oh no…' she whispered pointing to the top right of the document. A small circular symbol had been stamped atop the page, within the symbol were two crossed keys.

'Well that's put a Kybosh on it then…' snapped Cortez angrily. 'Whatever was down there has been *cleansed* by the Catholic Church.'

'Wait…' started Genevieve, her eyes lighting up. 'The church. The open eye symbol.' she scrambled in her bag for something, 'Do you remember last year we went to Malmesbury in Wiltshire? You recall the flying monk?' she asked.

'Eilmer the Benedictine monk who thought he was Daedalus?' laughed Cortez. 'Yes, why?'

She pulled out a small zip wallet filled with brochures from museums, churches and exhibitions that she had attended. She grinned once she found the brochure she was after, 'Eilmer, the first man to fly, five hundred years before Da Vinci and a thousand years before the Wright Brothers. He jumped off Malmesbury Abbey roof after tying wings to his hands and feet. He succeeded in flying for over a furlong before crashing down to earth breaking both legs, becoming lame. He then moved to the country's capital Winchester to aid in the management of the King's library.' she handed the brochure over to Cortez who glanced at it.
'The mediaeval historian William of Malmesbury wrote about it some years later, he may have even met Eilmer and received a first hand account. William famously wrote that the daring monk reportedly never blinked after the experience, that his eyes were permanently open from being illuminated from being closer to God than any other man.

What is more, Eilmer used the open eye symbol as a way to recognise his works and studies.'

'Am I right in thinking that he was around at the same time as Edward the Confessor?' Cortez raised an eyebrow.

'He was Edwards chief librarian, and would have had unprecedented access to the manuscripts there.' smiled Genevieve. 'Including the Lindisfarne Gospel. He would have also been privy to the works undertaken at Westminster.'

'But how does he link with the stones?' asked Cortez. 'And why would he hide it in that particular book?'

'Eilmer would have most likely read the surviving Lindisfarne Gospels, he would have learnt how to copy their Insular art style. He would have read all about the melting pot of Anglo-Saxon England at that period. He would have known about the integration of cultures and cultural traditions. These Gospels detailed the very history of the Celts, the Romans, the Byzantines, and the Copts, in Britain.' Her dark eyes gleamed with excitement.

'What are the chances that these Gospels also held the details of the stones?' added Cortez.

Genevieve's eyes lit up once again. 'There were pages missing from the Gospel. When I was at the museum I noticed that several pages had been removed from the beginning of the volume.'

'What if Eilmer was the one who removed them?' started Cortez. 'He was ordered to destroy certain information, but wanted to ensure the knowledge was retained, so he hid a message within the surviving pages? A sort of palimpsest within the original document.'

'The mention of the monoliths…' she started earnestly, 'They must have been significant.' She was absorbed in deep thought, shaking her head defiantly, trying to regain the momentum of the excitement they had felt only moments before. 'Why were these stones so important?' She paused, her mind racing around for an answer. She grinned and slumped back into the worn sofa taking up her phone. 'I will take west, you take east. Look for anything with a mention of standing stones, monoliths or anything ritual, ancient or Pagan that looks of interest.'

Cortez nodded in acceptance and clicked his knuckles in anticipation. He knew this was going to be a long one.

*

Cortez yawned and stretched out his strong arms. He looked up and out of the window to notice the afternoon had turned to early evening as the bell ringers from St George the Martyr in Southwark started their practice session.

'So, the present Cathedral, notably the paragon of Britain's most celebrated architect Sir Christopher Wren, is at least the fourth to have been built. It was built between 1675 and 1710, after its predecessor was destroyed in the Great Fire of London.' Cortez scrolled through his open DuckDuckGo DarkWeb browser pages and stopped.

'Christopher Wren…' replied Genevieve nodding. 'He was founder of the Royal Society. It may be worth checking out their records as well. Good idea Cortez.'

'That isn't everything. I did some digging around. You know via Tor… Clandestine stuff.' He looked to the door apprehensively as he spoke as if half expecting GCHQ to come crashing through at that very moment.

'And it looks like someone else has been looking into these stones, someone that you and I know very well.' He paused, adding drama to an otherwise normal situation. 'You remember Flint from the Cambridge job?'

'The old conspiracy nutjob?' Genevieve half laughed, recalling the old man that alleged to have been kidnapped by aliens whilst performing a ritual at Stonehenge several years ago. 'What has he got to do with this? You know I don't go for conspiracies.' she asked in trepidation, not certain she wanted to hear the answer.

'Well, you know what they say? All conspiracies have an essence of truth somewhere. Same as myths and legends… Majority of them are true. It looks like Flint might have actually been onto something.' Cortez rubbed his hands as he spoke. 'He stated St Paul's sat upon an old Roman temple.'

'I know for a fact no Roman remains have been found beneath St Pauls.' barked Genevieve, shaking her head at Cortez's comment.

'Flint has also written a paper on an alternative history of England. He mentions a unique stone causeway that runs the length of the country. His theory is that originally one hundred and eleven standing stones stood marking a perfectly straight road running from Winchester the Saxon capital of England to Colchester, one for each mile. Much like the Romans made mile markers that were used until 1963 when all British roads were standardised and the road signage system was created by Jock Kinneir and Margaret Calvert. Sadly, most of the ancient mile markers were scrapped, reused to build farmers' walls or simply thrown into grass verges along the road.' Cortez sipped his tea and licked his hairy lips.

'It is not known who designed or constructed this ancient road, but Flint alleges that it does predate the Roman road network. He even speculates here that the Romans used the preexisting standing stones as their mile markers, hewing them down to size and removing the petroglyphs from the facings.' Cortez leant in tapping furiously on his keyboard and clicked the map he had just created before zooming in on the centre of London. The thin blue line he had superimposed on the map ran straight through Westminster, Waterloo, and Blackfriars and up to St. Paul's Cathedral. Zooming out again it showed a conventional line running from Winchester to Colchester with small dots showing every mile. 'Well blow me...' He smiled joyfully.

'But hang on, look.' Interrupted Genevieve tapping the screen indignantly. 'The alignment misses St. Paul's completely. Your little dots are way off. This map states that it is only 1.68 miles between St. Peters and St. Pauls. Not two miles as Flint states, so the mile markers theory is incorrect and this little conspiracy is clearly flawed.' Genevieve's eyes flared as she looked at the maps on the screen, her busy brain taking it all in.

Cortez's face erupted as his chipped teeth appeared through his gaping bushy beard. 'Oh yea of little faith Genny, two very important factors to consider. One, the river "Thamesis" as Caesar called it was much wider back then... With the north bank being roughly in line with the Strand and Trafalgar Square. And the south bank shows Southwark as being under the river. And it ran a much different course than today.' he laughed heartily making his gold chained chest wobble. 'Look at this.' He turned back to the monitor and clicked his mouse, 'Ta-da.' He said dramatically as the image shifted around the blue line.

The river moved and widened as the meander changed as it twisted and contorted as it was digitally transported back in time. The island shape appeared around the image of Westminster and St. Pauls moved entirely to the northwest. 'St. Paul's was originally built in 604 AD, it was built by Mellitus, the Bishop of the East Saxons. It was a simple wooden church dedicated to St Paul built near the sand banks of the Thames. Flint states the first church was built around an old Pagan stone monolith that was integrated into the structures nave just like the one found at Waterloo taken to Westminster.

It burnt down in 675, and again in 962 during a savage Viking raid. The third church was built in stone and the plinth was covered in the more popular flagstone, but after another fire and some problematic flooding they decided to move and rebuild it further south on a more solid foundation. It wasn't until 1087 that the Normans managed the structural triumph and was completed, having in 1240 built the longest and tallest Christian church in the world. But what most people don't realise, according to Flint, is that St Paul's is nowhere near where it was originally built.'

Genevieve's eyes lit up, 'They did say they found no trace or evidence of a Roman Temple at the site...' she paused holding her chin, 'They were looking in the wrong place. Can we locate the original church?'

'I can get a rough general location from the original route line and distance from St. Peters and Blackfriars but London has changed a lot and we will be looking at nearly twenty feet of new build and development.' He paused for a moment, then tapped his monitor. 'The Cannon Street milliarium...' he said softly as his large finger ran north east along the line.

'I recall reading about this a few years back. Here it is, the Lundene Stane...' he read aloud from his screen. 'Now residing in the Museum of London. It had sat for years behind an iron grille in the wall of 111 Cannon Street, a dilapidated 1960s office building now long since demolished, originally stood towards the southern edge of the mediaeval Candlewick Street which is now Cannon Street, opposite the St Swithin's church called 'St Swithin at London Stone' by at least 1557, blah blah blah...' he pointed back to the monitor.

'An ancient limestone block damaged by the Great Fire of 1666 believed to have been used in all manner of mysterious, pagan and ancient rituals.' He sat back into his large ergonomic swivel chair again making it creak under his large frame, he held his arms up behind his scruffy head of hair and blew out his cheeks. His thick bushy beard split apart revealing his teeth as he grinned wildly.

'If we know that the next stone along from Westminster was on Cannon Street, then that would mean that the next stone, or shall we say the original location for the first wooden structure of St. Pauls was built somewhere approximately here...' he continued to tap on his mapping program until it displayed the thin blue line from Westminster Abbey, along to Cannon Street then up another mile to Spitalfields. 'In the vicinity of Spitalfields.' He continued to type as he spoke. 'The oldest building in the area is a Charnel House. It falls perfectly on the predicted line. We should drop by and have a little look around.'

'This is brilliant news Cortez! I could kiss you-' she paused as her mobile began to ring. Turning around she failed to see her old friend pucker up in a mix of jest and disappointment.

'There is the second factor that I need to tell you about, the measurement of the mile-' continued Cortez before he was cut off by Genevieve holding up her index finger to stop him.

She did not recognise the telephone number but she answered anyway, the majority of her work stemmed from withheld numbers or ex-directory lines. 'Genevieve Silankis,' she spoke clearly, waiting for the caller to speak.

'Miss Silankis?' came a quiet well-spoken female voice, just louder than a whisper.

'This is she.' She replied patiently.

'I have heard a great deal about you and your reputation. I was hoping that we could meet.' The voice paused as someone else spoke in the background, unmistakably a male. 'Would you be able to meet tomorrow afternoon, in London? I have something to show you.'

Genevieve took down the details and hung up her mobile telephone, turning back to Cortez who had at that moment started tapping away at his keyboard. 'You free tomorrow?' she asked him with a raised eyebrow.

'We goin' fishing?' he smiled back. 'You know I am a catch and release kinda' guy?'

'I know full well you were listening in on that call Cortez,' she spat back, slapping his arm playfully, 'So… Are you free?'

'For you Genny, always.' he mocked a bow before bursting with laughter.

*

Chapter 3
The Meet

Covent Garden, London

They had decided to play it safe and meet somewhere public. Genevieve never went alone to someone's home and she never disclosed her home address. Even in the academic and Relic hunter world you still got creeps who fancied giving stalking and harassment a go.
Genevieve had taken to asking Cortez along as either a visible deterrent, where he would sit beside her and look menacing. Or, as a shadow. She felt safe in the knowledge that he would always be watching her from a safe distance and ready to pounce at the drop of a hat.

The day after their mysterious phone call she found herself sitting in the sunken courtyard of the Crusting Pipe in the very heart of Covent Garden in London's West End. A string quartet played beside the staircase and tables as dozens of locals and tourists alike walked the gangway above as they frequented all the high end shops.

She was approached by a stick thin woman possibly in her late sixties or early seventies, well kept, tidy and surprisingly stylish in fashion donning a sleek black dress, but what Genevieve predominantly noticed was that she had hauntingly gaunt and sallow eyes. She wore an expression of constant surprise as though she had seen a ghost and became stuck with the shocked expression. This wasn't helped by her pencil thin eyebrows that had been drawn on rather high up her forehead.

The woman in black joined her at her table sitting opposite her. She held her hands together upon the table with fingers interlocked. Her hands were gloved, Genevieve thought this a little odd considering it was mid summer, but forgave her eccentricity and allowed a gentle smile.

'I am Genevieve Silankis, pleasure to meet you, Mrs?'
'My name is Nicola Stirling. Thank you for meeting me Miss Silankis,' started the old woman again in an almost whisper. Her intense eyes moved over Genevieve's face, eyes and hair. 'Your reputation precedes you Miss Silankis, this really is a privilege.'

'Thank you, it is always nice to hear my work being appreciated.' replied Genevieve coyly. She could feel her cheeks reddening. 'You mentioned you wanted to show me something?'
'I will not waste your time Miss Silankis, but I have heard that you would be able to help me. You have come highly recommended and I believe this is your area of expertise.' The woman in black retrieved a small manilla envelope from her bag and placed it onto the table between them. Genevieve pulled it towards her and opened the lid to have several photographs partially slide out. She took them out and looked them through before looking up, speechless at the woman in black.

'How did you-?' asked Genevieve, now very ill at ease.

The woman in black cut her off laconically with a wave of her hand as though she was shooing a fly. 'That is not important for now. What is important is what is in these photographs.'

She placed a gloved hand gently onto Genevieve's wrist, her stare intense. 'The secret is real. The stones are real.' She spoke slowly and quietly. She shifted her head left and right before continuing, 'My family have been tracing these stones for years. Our family home, Boreham House in Chelmsford contained several of these Bronze age Menhirs or monoliths. My ancestors discovered them and integrated them into a family mausoleum within the grounds.' She looked up to the steel and glass ceiling far above them as her eyes began to well with tears. 'Our family found themselves in several dire positions and subsequently have had to sell off the majority of the surrounding land. As a by-product of this lingering financial event the family mausoleum that is situated away from the main manor has just been sold off and is scheduled to be dismantled to make way for an industrial estate of all things.' The woman in black was visibly distraught and saddened by the reckless actions of her ancestors. She pointed to one of the photographs still in Genevieve's hands. 'You can see the markings? The petroglyphs, the three ringed Triskelion markings, the stars above the cup and ring markings and the animals that have been engraved upon the stones, immortalised in these ancient monoliths.'

Genevieve looked closer at the old photographs but what caught her eye was the small circle that had been bored through the solid plinth approximately three quarters of the way up the long face of the stone. 'Do you know what these holes were for?' she asked, pointing to one of them.

'Way finders…' replied the woman in black again in an almost whisper. 'It was said that those using the stones would walk from one to the next. But when it is dark or foggy, one could look through the hole and see the next stone. The next stone acts as a beacon.'

Genevieve frowned as she looked again at the photograph. The woman in black could see her mind working out the images. So she answered pro-actively, 'Each stone had a low fire burning in front and behind it, effectively illuminating its silhouette to those travelling in the dark of night.'

'What was the significance of Winchester and Colcheter?' she asked before she could stop herself.

'It is not the current buildings of the Great Hall in Winchester, and the Great Hall Keep in Colchester, but what lies beneath them. As you will soon come to discover, many other ancient sites make all of this so significant my dear.'

'Ancient civilisations used a series of paths to traverse this island.' started the small woman, 'A series of routes spread across the land in perfect undeviating linear lines. At interesting or crossing points great temples were erected. For example, the path north west from Winchester to Dearleap, if you follow that for twenty miles, or twenty stones you come to a significant crossing with paths to the south west, west, north and obviously back east to Winchester.' The old lady smiled at Genevieve playfully as she raised an eyebrow, 'I don't want to embarrass you my dear, but how is your geography?'

Genevieve placed the photographs down and smiled back, 'Well, twenty miles west of Winchester would bring you to...' she paused as she realised the location. 'You don't mean?'

'Yes.' replied the old woman in black with a serious nod. 'The most famous Bronze Age monument of the South, Stonehenge.'

She pulled out a map of the British Isles and handed it across for Genevieve to examine. 'You will soon discover a recurring theme, the majority of castles, manor homes or church buildings lie atop the original routes all across England. Wales is a different matter but that is due to the church having less power there.' The woman in black pointed at the hand drawn lines sketched upon the map with a thin gloved finger. Genevieve could see the points highlighted with a small dot, Winchester, Colchester and several others that appeared to make a symmetrical pattern across the map face heading in all directions.

'Fifty miles due north of the Great Hall in Winchester the path runs through Eynsham Hall off the A4095, North Leigh, Witney. Then up to Beacon Hill, an extremely significant site to the Bronze Age tribes. The path originally ran straight through here and many stones are still within the foundations of the Highclere Castle and The Heaven's Gate.' She paused for a moment to allow all of this to sink into Genevieve's visibly troubled mind. 'The path ran all the way up to Stoneleigh Abbey and Kenilworth castle.' she paused again. A look of disappointment covered her face. 'Sadly, from here all known knowledge of the stones going further north has been deleted from history.' She appeared to be reinvigorated as she continued to speak, her gloved boney finger once again above the map. 'Exactly fifty miles from Eynsham is Arbury Hall, Nuneaton. And it's now a derelict neighbour Astley Castle. You will note Atherstone, meaning After stone. But we will come back to that later. Now here is the part where you need to listen.'

'This route from Winchester,' she traced one line across the map, 'Led straight to Maen Bredwan Standing Stone Megalith in the west. This route,' again she traced the other direction from Winchester to Colchester.

'And this one,' she moved her hand from Colchester up to Astley Castle, 'And finally, Kenilworth castle to Maen Bredwan. All four routes, marked by ancient monoliths to guide the faithful, are exactly 111 miles long.'

'111 miles north-west from Winchester is a village called Wick, and guess what it is famous for?' Genevieve shrugged her shoulders, ancient sites and geography were her passion, but she honestly didn't know the answers to the old lady's questions.
'Tinkinswood and St. Lythans which are Neolithic burial chambers. At one of the major crossing points lie two significant locations, to the north of the pathway lies Maes Knoll Tump, an Iron Age hill fort in Bristol, and to the south of the pathway lies Stanton Drew Circles and Cove. There was an ancient stone bridge that crossed what is now the Bristol Channel, between Clevedon and Cardiff. Of course, five thousand years ago the ocean was a lot lower than it is today. This pathway then led to Maen Bredwan standing stone Megalith near Swansea and Nantgaredig.'

Genevieve could see that all of these points ran in a perfectly straight line across the map. There was no denying that these ancient sites did indeed follow the same path.

'There was another route that ran north from what is now called Lyme Regis, the original coastline now lost to the sea, that ran up through Glastonbury Tor, Dearleap standing stones, Stanton Drew, Hetty Pegler's Tump and Nympsfiled Barrow Belas Knap long barrow to Hailes Abbey. Can you guess the distance between these two points?' she asked rhetorically.

'One Hundred and eleven miles?' replied Genevieve.

'And the other side, Kingley Vale north of Chichester in West Sussex up to Hailes Abbey. Can you guess the distance?'

Once again Genevieve muttered, 'One Hundred and eleven miles?'

The more locations the old lady mentioned, pointing to each on her map Genevieve could see the clear orientation and layout across the country. 'So you have discovered an ancient highway system of sorts. Do you believe the pathways to be ritual?' exclaimed Genevieve excitedly. The woman in black nodded slowly, 'More ritual than you can imagine.'

'Mrs Stirling… Nicola, this is incredible, how many people know about this?' asked Genevieve earnestly.

'That is why I have come to speak to you.' said the woman in black despondently. Her entire body appeared dispirited. 'What you have discovered in the Lindisfarne Gospel texts is an ancient conspiracy that is linked to these very roads.' she again tapped the hand drawn map on the table.
'How do you know about the gospels?' spat Genevieve brusquely. The sudden wrench of sickening suspicion filled her stomach as she eyed the stranger.
'These roads have an important history,' continued Mrs Stirling as if she hadn't heard Genevieve, 'A history that entwines our ancient ancestors, the Romans, Edward the Confessor, Christopher Wren and ultimately the Catholic Church.'
'Mrs Stirling please.' retorted Genevieve authoritatively holding up a palm. 'How did you know about the gospel texts?'

'Footprints.' She answered seriously, tapping her gloved hands on the table. 'Digital footprints to be precise.'

'Mrs Stirling,' began Genevieve shortly, 'Before we go any further may I ask how you knew about our interest in these stones, and how you know about the…' she paused lowering her voice, 'Lindisfarne Gospel?'

'As I mentioned Miss Silankis, you came highly recommended and as such, We have been keeping an eye on you.'

'We?' asked Genevieve, now very concerned, she looked around her as she spoke.

'We, my daughters and I.' She started leaning forward. 'We placed you under observation, to ensure you were the correct person for the task ahead. We monitored your footsteps, your digital analytics and thus the geo-based traffic analysis to see what else you were doing. That is when we found the images of the gospels that you sent to your associate.'

'You hacked me?' spat Genevieve indignantly, rather taken aback. Genevieve shot a glance up to Cortez as they exchanged a lost expression, but she remained silent not wanting to give away his presence.

'We *monitored* you.' Replied Mrs Stirling gently, trying to make the act sound less intrusive.

'Monitored? Right, where I come from, it's called hacking. Which is very illegal, Mrs Stirling.' snapped Genevieve indignantly. Enraged by the betrayal that had just been disclosed to her so flippantly. The old lady waved a gloved hand dismissively fainting a shrug of her bony shoulders.

The old lady wore a serious expression. 'Be reasonable and think logically about this Miss Silankis. It appears that you too are searching for what has been hidden for millennia.' Smiled Mrs Stirling. 'So, we believed it best to ask for your help. Two minds are better than one, as they say.'

Genevieve frowned hard, her mind deep in thought as she raced through what had just been relayed to her. What had been disclosed to her was unbelievable, the theory, for that was all it was at this point was beyond anything she could have imagined. An ancient system of pathways around England, but what was their purpose, who had built them... And more importantly what was their secret? She sat in absolute silence as the intrigue filled her very soul. Her suspicions of the lady in black kept her on edge and she didn't know if she could even trust the old woman but the information she had just been told took precedence, and her overactive imagination was going wild. She decided to play along, to see what she could get from the mysterious old lady. 'I will hear you out.' retorted Genevieve.

'The Romans documented a lot of their campaigns and the lands they invaded, but England has always been a moot point regarding documentation or records.' started the old lady as Genevieve continued biting her lip.

Mrs Stirling hung her head and exhaled heavily before looking up directly into Genevieve's eyes. 'My family are currently in possession of an ancient text that details several stones just like the ones we have in the family mausoleum. I also have a photograph of where one of the stones had been defaced by a Roman soldier. An ancient form of graffiti if you will.'

She selected one of the photographs from the table nodding gently. 'Here.' She handed it over and pointed to a specific marking upon one of the larger stones built into the mausoleum wall, 'Four lines of Latin. Seldom used by the Celts of Alba 12,000 years ago.'

Leaning in over the photograph, Genevieve tried to read the inscription, she had studied Latin at school and later again at university but it definitely was not her forte, but she attempted a modest translation. 'FAS EST AB HOSTE DOCERI, "One should learn even from one's enemies", SIC ITUR SAXUM AD ASTRA "Such is the Stone path to the stars," HOMO ENIM FRUSTRA INTRAT IN LAPIDEM, "For men to enter or follow the milestone is in vain." VERITAS UOS LIBERABIT, "The truth shall make you free". DAEA "Goddess".
She sat back and re-read the inscription. 'Stone path to the stars?' she repeated under her breath.

Her thoughts were brought back to the present moment as the old lady's mobile telephone rang. The woman in blacks' eyes flared as she answered, she looked up to the gangway above as a young sharp dressed man hurried her up with a simple hand gesture.
'Is everything okay Mrs Stirling?' asked Genevieve apprehensively.
'I must away, we are not safe here.' the woman in black stood suddenly knocking the table sending the photographs to the ground. Genevieve bent down to pick them up but as she resurfaced Mrs Stirling had gone, and she was now alone at the table.

'Nicola?' she called out but there was no sign of the old woman. Looking up she noticed Cortez had also left his perch above them and was now nowhere to be seen. Her pocket buzzed as she took out her own phone half thinking it was Mrs Stirling explaining what was happening, but it was Cortez.

'She is making her way out through to Russell Street with two young men, they look messy. Probably private security by the look of them.' came the familiar voice of Cortez. Genevieve shoved the photographs into her satchel then ran up the stairs to the ground level, pushing her way past the crowds with her phone pressed to her ear. 'She is getting into a black Mercedes parked outside of Tuttons.' came Cortez's voice.

Genevieve sprinted out to the collonaded shopfronts outside of Covent Garden as she saw the car pulling away at speed. She cursed under her breath pushing her hair back behind her ear. 'Damn it!' she shouted. 'Can we follow her?' she asked hopefully into her handset.

'Nah, she's gone.' replied Cortez as he walked up behind her placing a reassuring hand on her shoulder as he lowered his own phone. He puffed out his cheeks then pointed to the restaurant. 'Lunch?' he asked with a smile as they walked into Tuttons.

*

Chapter 4
The Greet

Outside Tuttons, Covent Garden, London

Massimo stood behind one of the large stone pillars as he watched Genevieve and Cortez enter the restaurant across the road beneath the red fabric awning attached to the exterior wall of the building. Sucking his teeth he turned and walked back under the colonnade away from them as he processed what he had just seen. He closed his eyes bringing each of them into his mind's eye as he began *processing* them in what he called his *Hostile Reconnaissance*, a self taught method of evaluating and assessing the foreseeable hazards linked to an asset or enemy by reviewing previously provided intelligence, information or their physical appearance.

Target One: Nicola Stirling, 63 year old female, height: 5′ 7″, English, well educated, wealthy (Old money), widow, weakness - Family sentiment, vulnerable and old age. Risk: *Private security - Confirmed Armed* he noted.
Target Two: Genevieve Silankis, Historian, 30 years old female, height: 5′ 10″, accent heard (not English, maybe North European), athletic, smart, cute. He paused as he looked back towards the restaurant before smiling to himself as he continued walking away. Risk: low / medium.
Potential Target Three: Heard name of 'Cortez', occupation unknown, height: 6′ 4″, late 30's male, English, friend or partner, looks very strong, nice arms, Risk: medium / high could be a possible threat.
He flicked through the photographs he had just taken on his mobile phone, first was Stirling as she was escorted out to her waiting vehicle, he could see the pistol butts beneath the suit jackets of either man as they frog marched her across the square.

Next he looked at the vehicle itself, Mercedes-Maybach S-Class black with a private number plate, "NS 2".

Flicking through he came to the photographs of Genevieve as she ran after the old lady. He zoomed in on her face, her dark eyes fixated and determined. He paused longer than he normally would as he took in every detail of her attractive face. He looked up to see a street performer setting up in front of him so he diverted his course towards James Street away from the belly of the covered shops and restaurants. He examined the photograph of Cortez taking in his large bear-like build and muscular arms. Possibly ex-military, forearms look like a martial artist. He gave an uncensored huff as he placed his phone back inside his pocket. He had taken out hundreds of Cortez's in his time.

He walked quickly towards the glazed red brick frontage of Covent Garden's Underground station as he descended the busy mustard yellow tiled spiral steps. A short man in a hoodie knocked into him indignantly before raising an apologetic arm as he stalked off the other way. Massimo raised an eyebrow then tapped his pocket before frowning heavily. He turned and glided across the circular ribbed tunnel after the hooded man as they came to an intersection that led to another stairwell.

Seeing a discarded coffee cup on the ground he picked it up before looking all around him, no CCTV and one of those brief moments on the underground where you were completely alone, only to be swarmed by hundreds of people a few minutes later. He removed a silenced Jericho 941 from beneath his jacket and took aim at the hooded man before he whistled loudly. The hooded male stopped and spun around, his face dropped on seeing the firearm trained at his face only four feet away.

'I believe you have something of mine.' he whispered with a knowing smile. The hooded man searched his pockets frantically as he retrieved Massimo's telephone. The hooded man's hands shook with unadulterated fear as he handed it back to him. 'What is your name?' replied Massimo as he repocketed his phone, his pistol now lowered,
'Tyrese…' spat the hooded man short of breath and ashen faced.
'What gave you the impression that this line of work would benefit you?' asked Massimo openly. His dark eyes glaring maliciously. The hooded man just shrugged and looked pathetic.
Massimo re-holstered his pistol and stepped closer to the thief.
'Did your mother never tell you it is wrong to steal?'
'Sh… She's dead.' replied the pickpocket.
Massimo walked the man back against the tiled wall of the tunnel and shrugged, giving the "mano a borsa" pinched finger gesture, a sign infamous of all Italians. He stepped back laughing as the thief also gave a nervous laugh. Massimo's face dropped instantly as he punched the hooded man so fast he couldn't react, Massimo extended his middle knuckle striking the man's throat with a devastating force making him drop instantly, sliding down the circular walls of the underground tube tunnel with his head hunched forward. He leant over the fallen man and whispered, 'In Karate, this striking technique is known as Nakadaka Ken. It is used for disabling one's opponent.'

He placed the discarded coffee cup between the dead man's legs before throwing in some loose change. As he walked back through to the platform where a train was just pulling in, he boarderd it as dozens of passengers alighted and walked straight past the fallen pickpocket without a second glance, some even stepping over the dead man's extended legs with an irate 'tut' as he blocked the passage.

"The simple beauty of human psychology, 90% of people will intentionally avoid eye contact with a beggar or street vagrant." he chuckled to himself as the tube pulled away from the station.

*

Inside Tuttons, Covent Garden, London

'Well?' started Cortez as he tore a large piece of bread from the basket. 'What did we learn?'
Genevieve took up her large wine glass and swirled it vigorously creating a mini vortex inside. 'We learnt that this is going to be confusing, and that I am certain to have a headache by the end of the night.' She relayed the events of what Mrs Stirling had disclosed and showed him the photographs from the Stirling Mausoleum. She also showed him the small map detailing the stone line running across the country.

'How did they manage to hack me?' scoffed Cortez, 'Cheeky buggers.' He spat, gnawing another large mouthful of bread.

'Oh. That reminds me,' interrupted Cortez wiping a napkin across his mouth and beard of wine and breadcrumbs, 'I forgot to tell you earlier, the reason the format line didn't match up with the two mile distance between St. Peters and St. Pauls on the modern mapping system is due to the old English mile.' Genevieve just stared at him blankly.
'Ok, in summary,' continued Cortez, 'Back in Roman times they used the measurement of a thousand paces as a standard unit of length parameter. 1000 in Italian or Latin as it was is *Mille* where we get our word mile. So, 1000 paces becomes "Mille Passus".

In a modern English mile we have 5280 feet, or 63360 inches or 1760 yards. In an old English mile there were 6600 feet, 79,200 or 79,320 inches or 2288 yards which is the same as 1.3 international miles (2.1 km).'

'You've lost me…' replied Genevieve, sipping her wine glass, rubbing her head. 'Not all of us have doctoral degrees in mathematics, Cortez.'
'Right, the measurement varied… a lot, through history. But the measurements used in prehistory, way back then,' he said swiping his hands to one side of the table, 'Were a lot different to the measurements we use today.' he said, swiping the other way.

'But how do we know these were made in the Roman measurement and not some long lost quantification?' she challenged shortly.

'Because of Flint's theory about the Roman Milestones.' Cortez shot back, 'We know that the distance will be the same between each stone right?' he asked as she nodded back silently, 'So, if we find the two corresponding stones still in situ we can then measure the distance between them and plot out the entire route.'

'We could then find the exact location for whatever it was that Edward the Confessor discovered and see what is situated there today.'

'But we know it was between St. Pauls and St. Peters, we have been over this.' she snapped irritably.

'Well, whilst you were having your tête-à-tête with your mysterious friend, I was still working on Edward the Confessor trying to figure out what he has to do with all of this.'

He pulled out a small tablet and tapped the screen until his digital notes appeared. He placed a pair of reading glasses on his nose and peered down at the small screen held at arm's length.

'Edward was the son of Ethelred II "the Unready" and Emma, the daughter of Richard I of Normandy. He was exiled to Normandy for 25 years between 1016–1041 while the Danes held England under Sweyn Forkbeard and then Cnut. There are conflicting histories about the man but what is believed to be most accurate is taken from a Westminster monk called Osbert of Clare in the 1130's. He wrote a mini biography called "Vita beati Eadwardi regis Anglorum" which praised Edward for issuing prophecies, and a number of miracles, but mostly for building the Abbey at Westminster.'

'Life of the Blessed Edward, King of the English.' translated Genevieve as she sipped her white wine. 'I read about it yesterday whilst we were researching, a rather biassed review of the man from the opinion of the Church.'
'If you say so…' smiled Cortez as he peered back down his nose to the tablet screen. 'He battled the Danes, Scots and Welsh and really rattled the cages of Mercia and Wessex by introducing members of the Norman elite into Parliament and court.

He and Godwine, Earl of Wessex who held the most power in England have a barney, make up, have another barney. He marries Godwine's daughter, and they fall out again. He then has a few pops at Godwine's son Harold, but after more drama, Edward finally named Harold as his successor even though he'd promised the crown to his distant cousin, William, Duke of Normandy.

He died on 4 January 1066 and was buried in the abbey he had constructed at Westminster. William got the hump about Harold and we all know what happened later that year in 1066.' he put the tablet down and smiled across to Genevieve who was watching him with a pleasant smile. 'Like an episode of Eastenders innit?' he laughed.

'That must be the most paraphrased and bizarrely analogised history lecture I have ever witnessed Cortez.' she laughed softly.
'Cheers.' he smiled back at her, raising his glass of wine. 'Missed my calling as a lecturer didn't I.' he laughed heartily.

'Was there anything in Osbert's tome that mentioned why Edward built the Abbey on Thorney Island.' she asked, looking a little deflated.

'Well as it happens, listen to this…' he replied with a half-smile. 'It does mention a vision on Thorney Island by a fisherman, back before it was polluted and pumped full of human crap the Thames waters were well stocked with fish. It is said that St. Peter himself appeared before the young fisherman and demanded that a church dedicated to him was to be built on that very site of Thorney Island. The island itself got its name because it was full of tangled thickets of brambles, the old English words that end in 'ea' or 'ey' are related to islands, like Bermondsey, Battersea and Chelsea. So Thorn-Ey.' he looked up to see Genevieve's bright intelligent eyes staring at him intently.

She was fascinated in anything history themed. He decided to continue before he started to blush. 'The then King of London, an East Saxon called Sebert who had been a Pagan heard about this fishermans friend's vision and decided to build a little church there.

A Christian missionary called Mellitus, who was then made Bishop of London converted Sebert to Christianity meaning the Pagan church became the Collegiate Church of St. Peter. Obert states that Mellitus also saw St. Peter miraculously appear outside Sebert's church on the day it was consecrated. That's a coincidence innit? Just because it is written doesn't make it so.' he snubbed with a laugh.

Their meal arrived but they continued to talk as they ate, Cortez dove straight into his thick steak, chewing as he spoke. 'Whilst in exile Edward swore under oath that if and when he became King of England he would make a pilgrimage to St Peter's in Rome. This turned out to be impractical so the pope told him to build a church in honour of St. Peter instead. Edward then travelled through London during a terrible storm when he saw and took refuge inside the small Benedictine monastery that stood upon the island that was built by King Edgar and St Dunstan. The relentless storm damaged the lower walls of the monastery and Edward himself went about trying to fix them during the deluge and darkness. It is said that after he undertook the makeshift restoration of this site, he personally decided this would be the site of his church so he pimped up the small Benedictine monastery and voilà.'

'So, Edward himself didn't have the vision?' asked Genevieve, 'It seems to make sense but it is terribly impractical, why did he choose to build an Abbey there?' she shook her head in mild frustration. 'Why choose a regularly flooding marsh with poor clay soil with no natural building materials nearby? The site itself must have more importance than we know.'

'Or he found something underneath during the storm or later during the restoration works. Something that the church would provide a heavy purse for. To either protect or more realistically to keep silent.' smiled Cortez.

'And it has remained a significant focal point for the church ever since, either as an abbey or cathedral.' started Genevieve.

'About that, technically it's neither an abbey nor a cathedral.' finished Cortez with surprised eyebrows raised. 'Henry VIII converted the structure to the Church of England so it became a "Royal Peculiar" in 1560.'

Genevieve nodded to herself, 'The neighbouring Cathedral was only built ninety years ago and is completely separate to the Abbey.' she gnawed at her food, chewing determinedly as she thought. 'We should speak to a local historian, they will know more about the secrets of Westminster.'

'Funny you should say that Genny,' laughed Cortez humbly. 'I found out that they are conducting special tours of Westminster and took the liberty… You now have a date for tonight.' he beamed at her.
She raised her eyebrow quizzically, 'A date?'
'Would you do me the honour of joining me on said tour tonight at eight.' he leant forward and whispered, 'You remember Barcelona last year at the Basílica de la Sagrada Família?' he giggled. 'Where you and I snuck off during the late tour to search for the lost Dominican Rosary in the Chapel of Saint Joseph in the crypt? Well, let's try again tonight, see if we can find the stone plinth that was mentioned in the architecture notes.' he said jovially, inserting another huge piece of steak into his hairy mouth as he smiled broadly.
'You're on.' she smiled clinking their glasses together.

*

Beneath Westminster Abbey, London

Genevieve and Cortez walked slowly ensuring they were always dawdling at the rear of the group, taking photographs and touching the old stone walls and chatting to each other as the tour guide lapped up the other tourists undivided attention towards the front. Once they were deep enough into the older sections of the original Abbey they slipped off and away from the group. Moving quickly they entered the restricted area of the Abbey's Crypt and undercrofts. The low vaulted chamber smelt of ancient damp mixed with old plaster and decaying mortar.

'This is the only original and surviving area of the monastery from Edward's time.' spoke Genevieve sweeping her torch from left to right. 'Let's check all of these stones, maybe we can find what we are looking for in here.' She pointed to the floors with an excited smile.

They searched the floors and then the lower walls looking for the large stone, but the floors here were a jumble of Mediaeval and Tudor tiles with the occasional post-modern filling of concrete patching the ancient floor. They searched every inch of the crypt but there was no sign of the stone. They silently moved their way through the empty Abbey as they came to Britain's oldest oak door that led them into the Chapter House of Westminster Abbey. The room was a spectacular architectural design boasting a beautiful octagonal building with eight incredible stained glass windows set around a central column, oak seats ran along the perimeter with dozens of coats of arms adorning the magnificent woodwork. 'This room was the forerunner to the houses of Parliament where the King would address and counsel his Lords and the Barons.' whispered Genevieve. 'He would sit in the centre and allow his subjects to address him in turn.'

The two of them searched the room frantically moving up and down to locate the large stone. 'Nothing' huffed Genevieve with a dissatisfied pout. She did pause a moment to appreciate the glorious patterned flooring beneath her boots before she was hissed at by Cortez who was already by the door wanting to move on.

Off to the side of the east Cloister was the smaller Pyx Chamber, and although much smaller in size it was just as beautiful, its simplistic design the mastery of royal masons in 1250 it was used by Benedictine monks for their daily councils. It consisted of a small vaulted room with several uncomfortable looking wooden benches that sat before a cast iron barred window set above a simple crucifix and two large wooden chests in an alcove off to the right hand side. The flooring here was also a mixture of mediaeval and later tiles thrown together.

'No sign of a large ancient monolith.' sighed Cortez as he swept his torch along the plastered ceiling.

'We should locate the tour group and get out of here before we are-' started Genevieve as she hastily lowered her torch. 'Buona sera.' called a loud voice from behind them, making them both jump. Pointing their torches in the direction of the voice, but they could see no one.
'Who is there?' asked Cortez, squinting into the darkness.

'You two are very thorough, I must be honest… Your behaviour has me intrigued.' came the bodiless voice. The deep Italian accent echoing around the enclosed chamber. Genevieve and Cortez exchanged a brief glimpse, both nodding towards the door.

'Dove credete di andarre?' came the voice from the shadows as they made a dash for the ancient oak door. They froze on the spot as a tall, athletic man spun around the corner, dressed in a dark suit complete with a three quarter coat. In one hand he held a small torch that he shone in their eyes, in the other hand, through the darkness they could see the glint of a pistol.

He smiled sinisterly as he slowly approached them. His eyes twinkled in their torch light.
'Where do you think you are going?' he laughed as he ushered them back inside the Pyx Chamber with a flick of his torch. 'Over by the cross.' he demanded more seriously.
They edged across the dark room and sat down on one of the low wooden benches closest to the crucifix and barred window.

'Who are you?' asked Genevieve quietly, her eyes fixated on the stranger's gun. 'What do you want from us?' she spoke confidently considering her situation.

'Before that, I want to know what you two are doing in here?' spat the gunman, his dark eyes scanning the empty room. 'What were you looking for?' he enquired openly.

'We lost something earlier, so we came back to look for it.' answered Cortez. 'An earring,' he continued before he was cut off by the armed stranger who stepped closer.

The gunman laughed heartily and smiled widely. 'You are looking for something… In the dark?' he continued to laugh. 'Why not just ask the steward to help you, no?' he sneered menacingly. 'No, I know you are looking for something else… Tell me what it is.' He raised his pistol and pointed it at Cortez's large hairy face. 'Tell me now or I will end your life.'

Genevieve grabbed Cortez's muscular arm and squeezed. They looked at each other and nodded. 'We are looking for an old stone.' came Cortez simply.

'Più specifico… More specific,' smiled the gunman. 'We are standing in the belly of a one thousand year old church after all.' He looked around him to the ancient stone column in the centre of the room and ancient walls. 'Which stone?' He looked visibly more irritable and raised the gun to Cortez's forehead.

'A monolith… It pre-dates the Abbey by several thousand years.' snapped Genevieve holding Cortez's arm a little tighter.

'Tell me about this monolith-' started the gunam when several voices filled the Cloisters outside. 'Merda.' he spat under his breath. His eyes moved right to the two large wooden chests that sat open against the far wall. 'Inside… Rapidamente.' he hissed as he ordered them into the chest nearest the larger barred window. 'Not a sound…' he looked at them both shaking his pistol in his hand indicating what would happen, before he closed the large wooden lid atop them. He spun to his right hurdling the high sides of the second open chest. He ducked down just as the room became suddenly illuminated by the wall mounted lights as the tour guide entered cautiously flanked by two large security guards wearing matching white shirts, epaulettes, black clip-on ties and black peaked caps.

'When did you last see them?' asked one of the security guards to the flustered tour guide.
'About twenty, maybe thirty minutes ago…' he answered as they searched the empty room.
'And you're sure they didn't just get bored and leave?' snapped the other guard, his patience clearly tested.

'I don't honestly know… they were with the rest of the group one minute then-' he stopped as he saw the large chest across from him. He pointed a finger towards it and approached it apprehensively. 'This was open when the Abbey closed. They are always left open.'

Cortez saw their opportunity and coughed loudly, making the first security guard snap open the lid as he peered over the top at the two people squatting in the antique chests.
'Games up honey, they caught us.' said Cortez disheartenedly, standing up inside the chest.
'What you doin' in there?' snapped the second security guard as he joined his colleague. He looked inside for some form of incriminating evidence but found none.
'We were, um-' started Genevieve, also standing up. She suddenly took Cortez's hand in her own and snuggled up to him, pulling her shirt down around her waist. 'Trying something *different*… You know, to spice it up a bit.' she went red as she said it but she couldn't think of anything else to say.
'Yeah,' continued Cortez, a look of bewilderment all over his hairy face. 'I asked her if we could be a bit more *saucy.*' he trailed off as the security guards shook their heads disapprovingly, although one of them looked like they were trying not to laugh.

'In a crypt?!' shouted the tour guide in disbelief. His hands on his hips.

'Come on then you two lovebirds, out you get.' snapped the guard as he helped them both out of the chest. The second guard walked over to the second chest that still lay open and peered in over the top when he jumped back in astonishment, 'What the-!' he cried as the Italian gunman popped his head up resting his arms on the side of the second chest, resting his chin on top of his arms.

He shrugged limply shouting, 'Don't judge us for our indecorous and sordid sins!' he cheered playfully in an overly camp accent as he jumped out beside them. 'Please copper, have mercy on our ribald and sleazy souls.' he pleaded facetiously, holding his hands together in prayer as if to fight off being arrested. 'We are only human and we all have desires. What about you?' he said flirtatiously, touching the security guards clip on tie giving it a flick.

'Get out of it!' snapped the guard pushing the Italian over to the door.

The security guards and tour guide looked at each other then at the three of them.

'We will escort them to the security office and take their details," said the first security guard as they led them out of the Pyx Chamber. 'Come on then, away with you perverts.'

They were escorted to the North Great Door as the tour guide filed off down the cloister muttering to himself about inhumanity and disrespectful behaviour. Minutes later, with the door open the security guard took out his notepad and pencil ready to take their names. He looked up only to notice there were now only Genevieve and Cortez stood beside them.

'What the-' spat the second guard agog, looking around as he scratched his head under his peaked cap.

'Where did your *friend* get off to then?' asked the first guard as he too looked around the abandoned path and green either side. 'What's his name then?' he asked, holding his pencil ready.

'We don't know who he is, we only met him tonight.' answered Genevieve honestly. Only then did she realise what that looked like.

The guards exchanged another judgemental look before huffing loudly. They gave their details and apologised another dozen times before the security guards told them to clear off, not wanting to bother the fine officers of the Metropolitan Police.

'Don't come back for a long while.' laughed the first security guard.
'And keep it in the bedroom next time eh.' called the indignant second security guard as he closed the door on them with a slam.

*

'Jesus!' exclaimed Cortez. 'What the bloody hell was that all about?' he rubbed his fuzzy face, pushing his long scruffy hair back. He turned to Genevieve, taking her arm, 'Are you ok Genny?' he asked sincerely.
Genevieve nodded but her eyes were not on Cortez, they were too busy scanning the outside of Westminster for their *friend*. She looked up to see a small CCTV camera pointed at them perched high above a lamppost. 'Can you hack into that camera?' she asked as she started walking away down towards Parliament Square.
They climbed onto the nearest bus and made their way to the back seats, cautiously observing every person that climbed on after them.
'We need help, Cortez.' whispered Genevieve. 'Things are getting serious. That man was a professional.'

'I gathered that when I saw his shooter.' grunted Cortez seriously, cracking his knuckles, as he always did when nervous.

'If we can get a decent image of him from the security camera outside of Westminster then I can ask about to see if anyone knows who this mystery man is.' started Cortez. 'He sounded and definitely looked Italian. But who have we pissed off enough in Europe to warrant a visit from Mr Sleaze?'
'I can ask Mrs Stirling to see if she has any knowledge of this man,' replied Genevieve softly, again trying her phone. 'Still no answer.' she tutted irritably as she looked out of the window at the people walking past as they sat in the busy traffic.

'The cameras belong to the local council so it took me all of three minutes to get in through their firewall.' He turned his phone to show Genevieve the footage she wanted. 'Here you are dove. We should be coming out of that door any second.' he said pointing at his screen to the large north gate of Westminster. As he had stated the large door opened right on cue with the two of them being escorted out by the security guards, and more importantly the mysterious armed Italian. He paused the footage, zooming in on their nefarious friend taking several screenshots before the screen suddenly went black and started to buffer, 'Hang on… Somethings happening.' He turned the phone back to portrait to allow him to work out what had happened. 'Jesus…' he scoffed, slapping the back of the chair in front. 'Footage Deleted.' he read from the small screen, showing Genevieve. 'Looks like our Mystery man just wiped out the CCTV cameras digital hard drive for the area.'

Genevieve's mobile phone rang in her hand as they both exchanged a look, another withheld number, she tentatively answered, 'Hello?' she asked soberly, almost hesitant to hear the response.

'Miss Silankis?' replied a faint female voice. Genevieve held the phone to her chest and mouthed "Nicola Stirling" to Cortez so he knew who was calling. 'I must apologise for rushing out on you so suddenly, but you must understand that there are forces in play here that we cannot underestimate or take lightly,' the female paused as Genevieve heard shuffling papers in the background. 'I would like to ask you to come to my home so we can speak freely, before anything else happens.'

'Nicola,' Interrupted Genevieve shortly, 'I need to know who is after us, do you know anything about an Italian man?' She was met with only silence.

'Mrs Stirling, please. My friend and I were approached earlier this evening by an Italian man who had the intention of shooting us!' she shouted.

'Genny,' said Cortez cautiously, nodding to the other passengers of the bus. Genevieve huffed in frustration rolling her eyes but agreed and lowered her voice.

'Please… What are we involved in here?' she asked again. More silence then finally an answer.

'Come to my home tomorrow morning and I will explain everything to you.' replied the whispering voice. 'Where can my driver collect you from? Your home address?'

Genevieve paused, feeling deflated, 'I suppose you already know my address?' The awkward cough from Mrs Stirling was enough to answer the question. Genevieve agreed a time to meet the following morning before hanging up her phone. She gritted her teeth indignantly, slapping the shoulder of the seat in front causing a small plume of dust to lift up around them. Now she remembered why she didn't like public transport.

They alighted the bus at the next stop, it would be faster to walk at this time of evening anyway, they were nearly back to The Old Vic and the fresh air would do them both some good.

"Between Minsters East and West lies the King's secret confessors know best" spat Genevieve with her head in her hands as she sat at Cortez's cheap desk inside the security office. 'We need to head to the British Museum and look at the Cannon Street Stone.

'It closed at five Genny.' replied Cortez, tapping his large gold wristwatch.

Genevieve smiled at him, biting her lip. 'You dated that Archivist a few months back didn't you? The one who loved sushi and those Japanese Manga comics.'

Cortez's shoulders dropped, he knew what was coming. 'We went on two dates, that was it. She was a bit *possessive.*'

'Well...' started Genevieve mischievously, 'Might be worth giving her a call... See if she is working late tonight?' she replied with a raised eyebrow.

'You are unbelievable, you know that?' he cursed as he pulled out his mobile tapping the screen with his large thumb. He took in a deep breath and held the phone up to his chin as it began to ring.

'Claire? Hey, yeah it's me Cortez... Yeah that's right... How have you been?' he shot daggers across the room to Genevieve who smiled back at him as she started swivelling in his expensive desk chair. "You owe me" he mouthed to her as he listened to the Archivist.

'Yeah I know it's a bit out of the blue but I wondered if you fancied meeting up again. Are you working tonight?' he asked, closing his eyes. 'Great yeah, well. Would you like me to bring over some sushi and we can catch up whilst you work?' He scrunched his large hairy face up, shaking his fuzzy head. 'Great, yeah. I will see you at ten then. I look forward to it, see you soon. Bye.' he lay the phone down on the table and glared at Genevieve who was struggling to restrain a giggle.

'Well?' she asked. 'How did you get on?'

'You know full well how it went… This is actually cruel…
You know that right?' spat Cortez as he stood up. 'Putting her
hopes up like this…' He shook his head once more then
turned back to Genevieve, 'And you're paying for the bloody
sushi.' he shouted at her as she laughed.

The plan was simple, and a great success. Cortez arrived at the
British Museum with a large banquet of fresh sushi and some
soft drinks in hand. He was met by Claire at the back door of
the British Museum on Montague Place and then made their
way into the archives. She was middle aged, short, stocky yet
very attractive and insanely intelligent, but unfortunately, she
had several flaws in that she would become obsessed and
extremely possessive within a heartbeat, causing jealousy and
a manic distrust. Cortez just assumed she had been the victim
of heartbreak, but he enjoyed her company nonetheless.

With their shared interest in Japanese culture, cuisine, movies
and comics he had Claire swooning over him within minutes
and after they had dined and chatted for several hours he
excused himself to use the facilities. As he passed the service
door he swiped it open with Claire's access card that she had
given him so he could open the doors to the archives on his
return. The service door slowly opened to reveal Genevieve's
head and she popped through scurrying off the other way to
look for the Cannon Street Stone.
Cortez went back to finish his date with Claire returning her
access card who was none the wiser that someone else had
now surreptitiously entered the Museum.

Genevieve found the ancient stone standing on a purple
pedestal encased in a glass surround. A brief history was
displayed on the wall behind but it contained nothing she
didn't already know.

She set about making a 3D scan of the stone with the High Precision Revopoint scanner Cortez had given her earlier that evening. She walked around the glass case several times and then scanned the top of the stone. She really wanted to see if anything had been engraved or carved into the underside base of the stone but due to the glass it was unreachable. That and the fact that it weighed 76kg and although strong she would need Cortez's help to lift it to be able to get a successful scan. "It would have to wait." she told herself with resolve as she hurriedly made her way back to the service door before she was spotted by the patrolling security guards. She honestly didn't want to be found snooping around and thrown out of two of London's landmarks in the same day. Once she was outside she sent a text to Cortez and headed to wait for him at the English Garden Restaurant around the corner. The restaurant was open 24 hours a day. Perfect for shift workers and those dealing in clandestine operations in the middle of the night.

Cortez slumped down in the seat opposite her with a disgruntled and jaded frown, his dark eyes looked tired and shallow. Genevieve passed him a large glass of red wine and he inhaled it in one.
'Well?' he asked as he refilled his large glass from the bottle on their table. 'Did you manage to find it and get the scans?'
'No… Sorry I couldn't…' smirked Genevieve maliciously, 'You will need to arrange another date with Claire.' she laughed as Cortez just glared at her. She took out her phone and tapped the screen until Cortez's phone buzzed as it lit up on the table.
He opened the image on his Scandy Pro 3D app so that the ancient stone appeared on the screen as a high-definition mottled grey-white crystalline image covered in thousands of small dots.

Sitting in silence he rotated and gyrated the image on the small screen looking at all of the indentations for any possible writings or symbols. 'There is nothing here, it is too badly damaged by the gracious British weather.' he dropped his phone and took another heavy swig from the wine glass.

'How was the date?' asked Genevieve with a callous manner. Cortez looked at her sternly, 'You serious Genny? You busting my balls on purpose or are you just jealous that I haven't asked you out yet?'

Genevieve looked away awkwardly as she felt her cheeks redden. She sipped her wine and bit her lip. 'Sorry Simon... I-' She cut herself off now a little ashamed and conscience-stricken.

'It's fine Genny,' he paused as he looked at her intently, his smile was honest. 'It was good to see her again, but I'd rather have been spending my evening doing something else than using a poor girl so you can further your next adventure as a middle class treasure hunter.'

Genevieve met his eyes, that last comment had hurt her more than he'd realised. Cortez was unmistakably from a lower class family upbringing in East London and a somewhat *different* social background than hers, but his almost spiteful, bitter resentment of anyone from a more privileged or well off upbringing had a passion that she didn't understand. Something somewhere must have made him like this. But this was just one of his many secrets hidden away from the view of his closest friends.

'I am not a treasure hunter Cortez...' she whispered, her eyes misted. 'I'm a historian and archaeologist, explorer and antiquarian who happens to keep finding lost or forgotten treasures.'

Cortez laughed heartily, 'So how differently would you describe a treasure hunter then?'

'Fine,' she snapped back, sipping more wine defeatedly.

'Look, you did good with the scans.' He said tapping his phone on the tablecloth. 'I will take a look later to see if using more detailed resolution effects on the scans show up anything, alright?'

Genevieve nodded, holding her wine glass in both hands. She felt tired, the expired rush of adrenaline always came with the fatigue that made you just want to curl up and sleep. The strong wine wasn't helping the matter.

'When it quietens down a bit I want to check out Bishop's Square Charnel House.' started Cortez changing the subject. 'See if I can scan the area to get a decent look at what is down there. It crosses the path of our mysterious stone line. You never know, there may be some reference to the stars or some old alien message that has for some inexplicable reason been missed by the hundreds of archaeologists who excavated it.' he chuckled. 'Who knows, may find ourselves on an episode of Ancient Aliens one day.' This made them both laugh, and Genevieve feel much better in herself.

'Don't stay up too late Cortez, we have an early start.' She finished her glass of wine and stood up shouldering her bag. She leant down and kissed him lightly on the cheek, his wiry beard tickled her soft lips. 'Good night.' she whispered and they exchanged a small smile.

A light drizzle covered the windows of the Uber she climbed into. the driver chatted away to himself although she wasn't listening to a word he was saying. Her mind replayed the day's extraordinary events.

She snapped out of it when the vehicle stopped outside of her modest apartment, before she'd realised she was closing her front door and sliding across the security chain. Her body had acted on auto pilot, her legs muscle memory taking her up the stairs and into her home all the while her mind was distracted in deep thought.

She threw her bag onto her kitchen table and opened her fridge, its clinical pale white internal light lit up her otherwise dark kitchen. 'I need to change those damn bulbs…' she muttered irritably, reminding herself once again as she rolled her eyes to the blackened spent orbs protruding from the light fittings above her.

Back to the fridge the contents were still depressingly bare apart from several nearly empty condiment bottles, one of the down sides of a bachelorette's life spent travelling overseas. One seldom found themselves with groceries or in fact any edibles when you returned home. She looked to the fridge door to take out the milk carton, after a brief suspicious sniff of the contents by way of a safety check she flicked on her transparent glass kettle. The room swirled in the fabulous blue LED light from her novelty kettle as it rolled to a boil, she rubbed her tired eyes and made herself a strong coffee. She hadn't realised how much wine she had drunk with Cortez during dinner.

She settled on the kitchen table and removed the photographs of the Stirling Mausoleum from her bag, arranging them so that she could look at them all at once. The room now illuminated by her arrangement of lamps she set to work analysing each photograph in scrutinising detail. Three pages of her notebook now filled with lists and notes of everything she could see, taking note of all the tiniest markings, shapes and sizes of each of the large standing stones. Noting how the surface of each looked slightly different yet the overall size and shape were identical. All with the same small hole bore into the centre, three quarters of the way up.

Genevieve closed her heavy eyes and exhaled deeply as a stillness overcame her, her mind slowed and she felt a cold yet refreshing wind against her face.

Opening her eyes she found herself standing amongst dark trees surrounding a rich flat green marshland. Before her stood one of the large dark grey monolith stones. Easily ten feet tall and three feet wide, its surface carved with multiple cup and ring markings, red vibrant painted patterns twisted across its solid face. Several small animal skulls adorned the base in offer of tribute and sacrificial offering. Two smouldering pyres stood either side like sentinels allowing those on pilgrimage to see it after dusk. She approached slowly, her eyes level with the smooth round bore-hole in the thick stone slab's centre. Peering through like a spyhole in a colossal door she saw the well used track line made from the thousands of feet that had scarred the earth walking the same path. Smaller, simpler stones ran parallel with the footpath creating a concourse for the ritualistic route, leading all the way to the next large dark grey monolith just visible one mile away against the lush green background. The cyan blue sky above her suddenly grew dark as it was replaced with a deep inky-purple black that flashed into a speckled canopy of millions of sparkling stars. Stepping back in absolute amazement she covered her mouth at the sight. She had never seen so many stars in the night sky. She tried adamantly to recognise some of the constellations but no matter how hard she tried the heavens looked somehow foreign to her. Movement on the other side of the thick monoliths' spyhole brought her eyes back down from the twinkling light of the starry night sky. Coldness crept across her shoulders and neck as she hugged herself, fighting it off. Looking back through the hole to see what had caught her eye she recoiled at the appearance of the Italian Hitman standing on the opposite side, his silenced pistol raised and now pointing directly through the peephole.

*

Undisclosed Location

The tenebrous smoke filled room echoed from the voices below, 'Massimo has failed to stop the target,' said an irritable voice. 'They are likely now going to meet.'
'Hmm.' replied another. 'Your man appears to be slipping. You promised us his success.'
'The Wolf has never failed before, he will not fail now.' spat the third voice reassuringly. 'I ask that we give him more time.'
'There is too much at risk.' stated the first voice. 'We shall send in our own team to infiltrate the home's security team.'
'Agreed,' replied the other man. 'It bears repeating that we must not fail.'
The third voice remained silent.
'In eius luce et gratia.' they muttered as one.

*

Chapter 5
The Stones

Genevieve sat up with a start, her back and shoulders aching in protest from sleeping uncomfortably in her Windsor dining chair. Her phone was buzzing beside her as she saw Cortez's large face fill her screen.

She swigged her coffee and regretted it instantly pulling a bizarre face. "Erh, cold." she spat it back into the cup as she wiped her mouth with the back of her sleeved hand. Tapping her phone angrily to answer she bellowed,

'Cortez!' she shouted indignantly, 'Why are you calling me in the middle of the night?' she cursed under her breath as she stretched her arms up before windmilling them to get some blood and the sensation of feeling back into them.

'Two things...' started Cortez defensively via loudspeaker, 'One, I got a potential ID on Mr Sleaze. And two, it's 7 am, this is your wake up call.'

The hot shower had drastically helped Genevieve feel more human after her disturbed night's sleep and obscure dream. But the small brown bag of freshly made pastries and cup of steaming cappuccino Cortez had brought inside with him really sealed the deal. She threw on some clothes and joined him in her kitchen as they tucked into another pastry.

'I used the images we managed to take from the Council's CCTV to ask about to see if anyone knew who this man was, being sure to not make ourselves any more of a target I stated that I was looking to hire him. It transpires that our little friend has quite the history of violence. He is known professionally as "*The Wolf*" and he is bad news.' said Cortez solemnly, meeting Genevieve's eyes. 'Very bad news...' he repeated as he tore the head off his croissant. 'This guy is good, ex-military, ex-special forces and a contract fee that would make your eyes water.'

Genevieve sat beside him and looked at the Italian man's emotionless face from their snapshot outside Westminster. 'The Wolf? That just sounds creepy.'

Cortez nodded, 'His real name is Massimo Lupo, born in Rome and raised in Switzerland, Son of an influential banker, daughter of an heiress from old money. Lupo as you probably know in Italian...'
'Means Wolf.' answered Genevieve rhetorically, nodding. 'Is there any way we can find out who has hired him?' She asked encouragingly, her eyebrow raised.

'Genny, this is serious stuff. This sort of echelon of people don't publicly display who they work for. And I don't have the foggiest on how to even start looking to be honest with you. What I do know is that this man's fee is 250,000 Euro per hit. That means someone somewhere has spent half a million to take us out.' He scrolled his phone to show her another image. A grainy photograph of a portly sharp dressed wizened man with a dark moustache had his arm around a nubile model on a yacht somewhere in the Mediterranean.
'At first I thought it may have been our old friend Brooke from the Cambridge job last year trying to muscle his way in after he lost out on those Rosary Beads.' he said with a defeated huff, his large shoulders dropping several inches.
'But then I heard rumours of this man.' He tapped his phone screen, turning it so Genevieve could see it clearly.
'And who is he?' she asked quietly.
'More bad news...' replied Cortez. 'This is Armon Di Silva. Black Market Antiquities dealer to the nefariously rich and famous. You want it, he will get it for you... No matter what the cost or location.'
Genevieve leant in to take a closer look at the old man. 'I have never seen him before.'

'Not surprising really. He is a ghost, this is one of the only photographs of the man. Hence, it's really poor quality. I have heard that he once broke into the Vatican's most secure vault to steal an old Relic belonging to St. John The Baptist.'

'What was it?' she asked in surprise.

'His head.' he smiled back.

Genevieve nursed her coffee and racked her brain, 'Why would an Antiquities dealer want to hire a Professional Italian hitman to take us out?' she chewed the inside of her cheek as she thought. 'What can these old stones be hiding that would attract this much attention?' she continued shaking her tired head.

'I had a theory about that. What if these ancient stones, that resulted in Edward the Confessor being granted immunity, favour and a very large praise from the Catholic Church are linked to something potentially hazardous to them. What if these stones hold information that somehow challenges the ideology or very essence of the Church.' Cortez put the remaining half of his croissant into his large mouth, speaking with his mouth full, 'Now a millennium later, the Church has wind of people digging around the old stones once again. And not wanting to cause another schism, or the prospect of any new evidence to be unearthed, they hire Di Silva to acquire this item or knowledge for them, whatever it is. He in turn hires Mr Sleaze to remove any complications. i.e. You and me.'

'It's all very Da Vinci Code isn't it Cortez?' she half smiled. 'This has escalated very quickly.' whined Genevieve, putting her head into her hands. 'For the information about Edward to be hidden in Gospel texts and the stone causeways to hold this much influence over the Church there must be something we have missed. We need to see these stones and speak to Mrs Stirling to fully understand what it is we are dealing with.

Cortez put his phone down, inhaling deeply. 'About her…' he started. 'I spent some time looking into our mysterious contact, Mrs Stirling.' he added. His face deadpan and now far more serious than before. 'She has skeletons in her closet that will make you squirm Genny.'

He leant in closer, 'The gloves that she always wears, apparently she was tortured years back. After a failed business endeavour her family got into trouble with the sort of people you really don't want trouble with. Her parents and husband couldn't pay so they turned on her to make an example.'

'Jesus!' spat Genevieve across the table, 'That is awful!'

'What's worse is that after this, her family are forced to sell off most of their estate to pay off the debt.'

'Oh excellent,' she replied sarcastically, 'And there was me thinking for once we may be dealing with someone normal.' she downed her coffee as her intercom buzzed loudly.

'They're here.' said Cortez softly, his voice mocking the infamous Poltergeist scene.

*

Outside her front door stood two men in dark suits. One wore a smile, the other a frown.

'Good morning Miss Silankis, are you ready to go?' said smiles as he pointed towards the large immaculate Range Rover Evoque parked directly outside the apartment block.

The vehicle's cavernous interior was plush and extremely sleek, the leather was soft and stylish, the trim expertly designed and finished with several seldom seen additions that caught Cortez's keen eyes as he buckled up in the back seat. Genevieve noticed the small emblem on each of the tinted windows. A small winged lion holding a sword. The logo of the Canadian based company, Inkas armoured vehicles, the true mark of luxury.

Their escorts remained silent unless asked a direct question by Cortez or Genevieve which made the journey awkwardly uncomfortable. The two men scanned every passing vehicle, observed every overtaking truck, their demeanour only becoming more visibly relaxed as they exited the bustling roads of inner city London and continued through the sprawling open Essex countryside.

'So, I managed to swing by Bishop's Square Charnel House this morning, got a full 3D scan and managed to find some local archaeological group' dig reports from the MOLA database.'

'Anything interesting?' asked Genevieve quietly although there was no point trying to hide it from their escort sitting directly in front of them.

'When they removed the rubble from the Fire of London they discovered some interesting stones used in the foundations. Take a butchers down there, behind the third metal support prong holding up that section of the wall.' Cortez pointed to a small symbol etched onto the stone.

'Is it not just a masons mark?' challenged Genevieve looking at Cortez's image.

'The scan did pick up multiple pieces of masonry etched by the masons who wanted to secure the correct remittance from their hard labours.' he grinned, 'But this one is an Awen.' He zoomed in on the image so she could better see the marking. It was worn, faded and smooth but it was unmistakable. Three lines beneath three small dots sat carved onto an exposed edge of the foundation beneath the Caen stone and decorative knapped flints above.

'Its the correct size and shape...' added Genevieve softly. Cortez then changed the image to that of the 3D scan he had conducted. 'Now take a look at this.' He beamed,

The scan showed the wall and foundation stone beneath, the symbol was clearer on the digital display, as it removed the surface details and left only the contours and defects. But what it also showed was a small disturbance in the stones surface, roughly the same size as Cortez's palm was a mortar filled circle. 'Now watch this.' he said tapping the Density Calculator button.

The cement filled circle now resembled a tube running the depth of the stone, the circle was a filled hole within the ancient stone. Genevieve grabbed his phone to look closer, it was just like the one in her dream.

'We have arrived.' called the cheerful escort making them both look up.

Cortez looked out through the large car's front passenger window at an impressive gate house set back off the small road. A high metal filigree gate was flanked by large stone posts topped with stone spheres. The neighbouring cottage sat on the other side of the intimidating perimeter fence.

He whistled making a remark at how even the gatekeeper lived in a luxury home, his remark of it "looking cute" apparently fell on deaf ears to their silent escorts. It was the sort of place one would see on an ornamental biscuit tin or jigsaw puzzle. What you wouldn't normally see though was the three large men who had just walked out of the cottage's front door as their car rolled to a stop. Mrs Stirling's security detail no less, he thought to himself.

The large gate began to swing open as the car once again rolled forward.

'The gate-keeper's cottage.' Laughed the driver, 'Grade 1 listed building… Worth a small fortune.'

'It is beautiful,' smiled Genevieve as they drove past it.

'Wait till you see the main house,' laughed the driver. The second escort just huffed with a deeper frown as the gate closed behind them. The driveway disappeared over a crest in the low rolling green hills as they drove for what seemed like five minutes through the large grounds, past a large lake and several stands of trees. Finally the main house came into view. A spectacularly towered Gothic building that resembled a Jacobethan castle.

'Like Downtown Abbey, innit Genny?' spluttered Cortez, hunching down to see under the car's sun visor that had been hinged down by the grumpy escort in the front passenger seat.

The driveway split into two around a large central fountain and pond that acted as an ornamental turning circle for the residents and guests to drive around. Genevieve watched as four more men in suits stepped down from the grand front door, followed by Mrs Stirling and two younger ladies.

Alighting the large armoured car, Cortez and Genevieve were met with smiles and warm welcomes from their mysterious host. Her demeanour and manner relaxed and confident, the complete opposite from what they had witnessed the previous day whilst in London. 'Welcome to my home, please let's go inside.' She waved a gloved hand towards the door.

Inside the grand entrance hall stood an extremely large fireplace to their right, large enough for Cortez and all the security team to clamber inside. Either side stood ornate dressers that housed antiques and ornaments.

Opposite stood a solid oak staircase that dog legged off to the left and then left again taking you up to the first floor. Directly in front of them stood two large doors that led into a Georgian style parlour, with several chaise lounges, two very deep sofas either side of an oriental coffee table and a grand piano.

Mrs Stirling sat down as a tray of tea was brought over to them by one of the security detail. The four men stood around the corners of the room arms together in front of them, silent sentinels manning their posts. The two ladies that had stood with their host outside now sat beside her on the far sofa, Genevieve and Cortez's large frame taking up the opposite sofa.

'These are my daughters, Catherine and Anne.' Started Mrs Stirling, as they bowed their heads slightly in welcome.

'Thank you for inviting us into your home.' smiled Genevieve warmly. She glanced up at the walls, each adorned with artwork, paintings and photographs of Nicola and her two daughters. She noticed that none of the photographs were of her husband.

Cortez just looked around him at the sheer expanse of the building, all the furnishings and architectural details that made up the huge manor.

'Let us not dilly dally any further.' started Mrs Stirling strongly. 'The reason you are here.' she paused as she smiled at each of her daughters before turning back to their guests. 'My family have been searching for answers to the secrets hidden within the ancient stones that once ran through our very home. We have discovered old texts and poems that tell of the old routes marked by standing stones.' She looked up to the door to her left before continuing. 'These routes were used for thousands of years, the highways of the Neolithic and Bronze Age people.'

'They are relics of a forgotten world. A world before science full of mystery and magic.' interjected Anne, interrupting her mother. 'As science replaced alchemy and witchcraft in the fourteenth century, we too endeavour to solve this once ancient mystery using modern interpretation and understanding.'

'Several significant sites throughout Britain and Europe were linked by stone monolithic pathways. Masonry markers that follow the Ley lines across the country to aid travellers, druids and priests along their way.'

'But what were they for?' asked Mrs Sitrling solemnly. 'Let us show you. Follow me.' she said as she stood up and walked out of the parlour, followed closely by her daughters and the four henchmen.

'There has been occupation on the estate since the early 7th century. But mankind has been walking these fields for many thousands of years.' She pointed off to the far wall of the balconied office that looked over the library below.

The wall housed an old hand drawn map, charting the original grounds of the house in all its glory. 'The estate once consisted of nearly 5,000 acres. But during the early 19th century my ancestors had to sell off a large majority of it. Ill-advised investments and a disastrous penchant for gambling I am afraid.' She stroked the old map with her gloved hand, her eyes lost for a moment deep in thought or memory.

She snapped back releasing a smile, 'To the reason you are here' she said walking over to a large leather-bound photograph album sitting on the wooden desk behind them. Opening it she flicked through to larger prints of the ones she had given to Genevieve the previous day. But inside this large album were far more photographs of the old stones and the mausoleum, she stood back ushering them both forward.

Their eyes scanned over the images as they saw unmistakable carvings in the shape of the female form on the surface of the stones. There was also a sequence of vertical writings across several of the stones.

'Ogham?' asked Genevieve.

'Yes.' Nodded Mrs Stirling warmly.

'What is Ogam?' asked Cortez, scratching his beard.

'*Ogham*,' Genevieve corrected him, 'It is an ancient runic scripture for a Gaelic alphabet believed to have originated in Ireland at the turn of the first century, inspired by Ogma, god of eloquence. It is read from bottom to top.'

'What does it say?' he asked excitedly. 'I only speak English and Klingon.'

'No idea.' She replied modestly, shrugging her shoulders. 'Each glyph represents a tree or Feda. But I do not know how to read them.' She tilted her head and looked to the next photograph releasing a broad smile. 'But this I do recognise…' she tapped the old photograph. 'Old Norse, Lønnruner or Cipher Runes.'

'A famous Icelander named Jón Ólafsson penned a manuscript in the 18th century deciphering cryptic runes.' She stood taking out her tablet from her satchel. 'Whilst at Holy Island, Lindisfarne I spent some time recording similar cipher runes inside the castle, so I read his manuscript.' She paused, turning her device on. 'And this one…' she pointed to the photograph, laying down her tablet beside it. 'Is the same.' The digital image and the photograph were an identical match. 'This means that there is both a Scandinavian and Celtic context to the stones.'

'Very good Ms Silankis.' Called Mrs Stirling from behind them. 'The Ogham text tells of The Great Goddess. The pagan religion that was prolific across all of Neolithic Europe from 10,000 BC to 1,000 BC. It celebrated the divine feminine and rite of birth. Through the creation and continuation of all life.'

'Judging by the multiple markings and graffiti glyphs, the stone path was revered by dozens of invading people, traders and migrants for millennia.

That is until the Catholic Church arrived in 597 AD. By 650 AD they ordered *"Tabula Rasa"* on all pre-existing Pagan temples, shrines and altars, their campaign to ensure all ritual sites be destroyed and built anew in the image of their Neo male god.'

'Like the Taliban in the Middle East of today.' snapped Catherine.

'It is nothing new.' retorted Anne, 'All Empires erase the predecessor and instil their own ethos. Look at the British Empire, the Mongols, the Romans and the Greeks before them.'

'It is said that approximately 80% of all churches are built on the ruins of older religious sites.' continued Anne.

'St. Peters.' Said Genevieve to Cortez nodding.

Mrs Stirling also nodded in agreement. 'Edward the Confessor discovered the old stones, and he took the time to discover what they meant. To reveal their secrets. The House of Wessex were ignorant following the churches ethos of masculine heredity, the son becomes ruler after their father passes, in this case Æthelred the Unready. But his mother, Emma of Normandy came from a much older lineage, a lineage that accepted female equality. Her father Richard I of Normandy declared war on the Islamic East due to their extreme chauvinism against women.'

Catherine scoffed aloud, 'That and to exploit their mountains of spices and gold.'

'She had ensured her son Edward, and Harold after him knew of the old ways. Edward secretly built Westminster as a symbol to both the masculine and the feminine. He restored the Anglo-Saxon dynasty to the English throne by coming to an accord with the Danes who accepted and still held respect for their older Gods, and most importantly their female Gods. Much like Richard I's own Grandfather Rollo, a Viking who became the first Duke of Normandy.'

'William, unlike his grandfather Richard and his Great-grandfather Rollo, despised the idea of women in the church. This was due to him being raised and educated by the church, by his mentor the Milanese Pope Alexander II. On 6th May 1065, Pope Alexander held a special council in Rome, attended by William himself and at least eight cardinals and forty-three bishops. They were known as The Order of the Sun, or *Ordo Solis*. This council ordered their puppet William to invade England and crush Edward and Harold's blasphemous vision of an equal faith.'

'I thought the church gave their blessing to Edward to build Westminster?' asked Genevieve.

'They did. As far as the Papal institution knew Edward's intentions were to reinstate the hold over England through the traditional power of faith. If they had known of his "heretic sacrilege" as they later called it in correspondence to William, they would have had him executed.'

'But, the Church had an ulterior motive, control.' called Anne, 'Let Edward build his Abbey, install William as king of both France and England and unleash their plan.

To be able to control, silence and smother women and the Feminist opinion – ensuring all their power and dominance was removed from all society and handed to a few male supremacists, who were led by greed and thirst for power and dominion.'

'What did Edward learn from the stones?' asked Cortez.

'The stones marked a ceremonial route used in ritual for all females coming of age. They would walk the route with their families, as their ancestors had done before them to gatherings, feasts and celestial movements at key locations across the continent in alignment with solar, luna and astronomical events.'

'It wasn't just about a young woman's transition from adolescent child to adulthood. The importance came from the knowledge that was gleaned along the journey.'

'The Neolithic was an age of significant development, the birth of agriculture and social reform. The head of the family would learn how to farm crops, raise cattle, how to cook and provide for their family, how to manage trade and wrong doings. This was what was so important to the people of the world. United under one ideology the people lived in peace and prosperity for over nine thousand years, with everyone having the same access to education. The responsibility came down to one within every household… The Mother.'

'I have something else to show you.' called Mrs Stirling. She carried over a large leather bound file decorated with a thin leather strap and wooden toggles, the file was about four inches thick.

She placed it onto the low table as Genevieve noticed the old lady's wrists were scared just beneath the gloves that she always wore.She glanced over to Cortez, her mind relaying what he had said earlier about her being tortured as a consequence for her family not being able to pay off a debt.

Nicola coughed loudly, bringing Genevieve's eye up to hers. 'What do you know about the Great Goddess?' she asked openly.

'As in the Venus of Willendorf? A revered Neolithic deity from 30,000 to 25,000 BC.' answered Genevieve. 'A small limestone nude female form representing fertility found across europe.'

Stirling gave a knowing smile as she unravelled the thin cord that wrapped the wooden toggles and opened the large leather backed cover revealing dozens of large velum pages secured to thick parchment backings.

'In 1086 William the First made a record of all of England and Wales' residents, livestock, mills, farms and buildings.'

'The Doomsday Book.' Interjected Genevieve and Cortez together.

Stirling nodded politely, 'What is not known is that he also surveyed the majority of England's major cities and towns tasking his half-brother and long-time friend and advisor the Bishop Odo of Bayeux to document all religious sites along with written accounts of local legends and histories.'

She turned to the next page unfolding the protective greaseproof sheet cover. 'This is a page from one of Bishop Odo's reports. I will translate it from the mediaeval French,

'Eight standing stones standing half and one toise de l'Écritoire, ringing a central altar plinth, the seat of power.'

'Charlemagne's royal unit,' said Cortez matter of factly, 'It's the distance between the fingertips of the outstretched arms of a man. One and a half, average height back then was 5' 6" so thats about what, one hundred inches, approximately just over eight feet tall?' suggested Cortez, mentally visualising the stones in his mind's eye.

Stirling continued, 'Beside the west bank of the Isis along the Thorn pass. Now named the Chapter House.'

Genevieve looked up, meeting Mrs Stirling's broad smile. 'What?' she stood up to look at the old velum page as she scanned it with her eyes. 'The Chapter House is built on a Neolithic ritual site?'

Cortez scratched his beard nonplussed, 'How come we didn't see any of this during our research?'

Mrs Stirling lifted her head, her eyes meeting Cortez's. 'Bishop Odo goes on to say *"The stones lie along the solar line, once used by ancient Queens to speak the divine."* the divine being wisdom.' Continued Stirling.

'This document was only privy to the King and his closest council. This is, as far as we are aware, the only reference to the stone monument and the original purpose of the St. Paul's site from that period. The reason you or anyone else has not heard about this is because Edward the Confessor built his palace and abbey atop the ancient Neolithic meeting place. Eradicating the once significant ritual site of importance from history.'

'Miss Silankis,' said Catherine walking closer to her mother's side. 'The pages from which my mother is reading were discovered in 1705 beneath Kensington Palace during the reign of Queen Anne. After her death in 1714 the pages were placed into storage along with the majority of her letters and personal files and correspondence. When George Hanover took the throne the documents were forgotten about, not being able to read English he had little interest in them. They lay undisturbed until Sir Robert Walpole looted the royal archive for his own personal library after he was permitted as the first Prime Minister.'

'The documents stayed in situ until Spencer Perceval was assassinated in the lobby of the House of Commons in 1812. An understudy and close friend was our ancestor Sir John Tyrell who after some persuasion brought the entire contents of Perceval's library here to Boreham House.'

'What we are trying to say,' Interrupted Anne cutting her sister off mid-sentence, 'Is that there is no *"outside"* knowledge of these documents or their reference to an ancient female monarchy.

The Royal historians didn't start their auditing administration until 1199 with King John. Despite his failures as a leader, ruler or king he was a bloody assiduous archivist. He formed the very backbone of the record keeping systems in this country. Did you know he kept a daily register and record of every place he went to for his entire reign?'

Mrs Stirling was the one to interrupt her daughters now, 'These records became *for eyes only* so to speak. With the growing influence of the Catholic Church contradictory evidence like this would cause significant unrest.' She paused, a serious look upon her aged face. 'If the world knew that females once ruled over the lands, the Church's authority would come into question.'

'Ha, I knew the Catholic Church would be involved somewhere.' Spat Cortez from the sofa.

'Surely this would enhance the history of England, something that would outweigh the power of the Holy See?'

'Clearly you have not had any involvement with the Church.' Sneered Catherine with a raised eyebrow. Her eyes then looking across to her mother, then down to her gloved hands.

'For centuries the Church has used oppression and fear to control the people. Their word was literally gospel and to question it was heresy. A crime punishable by death. These documents have been hidden out of simple fear of retribution.'

Mrs Stirling sat back, relaxing into the low sofa, her gloved hands placed gently on her lap. 'The church held most of Europe in its hand, regulating and monitoring everything that was said, read and preached. The Church had agents in every country, spies in every royal court and agents belonging to the Spanish Inquisition at every level of hierarchy.'

'Nobody expects the Spanish Inquisition.' Laughed Cortez to himself, he soon silenced himself on seeing not one of the women present joining him.

'If even a whiff of Pagan, heretical or anti-dogmatic teachings were discovered one would be tortured and put to death often without trial.' Continued Mrs Stirling, unabashed as if she hadn't heard Cortez's comment. "Not even Henry Tudor had enough power to reveal these secrets, even as the head of his own Church of England. His daughter Elizabeth tried, going against the counsel of Wolsey. The anger of both King Philip and the pope resulted in the Spanish armada of 1588. Her father's audacious divorce to Catherine of Aragon and marriage to Anne Boleyn was one thing, but to attempt to disrespect and eradicate the church's power was too much of an act of insolence.'

Catherine chipped in, 'With the turbulence of the 16th century's religious persecutions between Catholicism and Protestantism the documents were hidden away. Well away from the damning eyes of 'Bloody' Mary Tudor and her attempt to restore Catholicism and the church's dominion. Ending up being discovered during Queen Anne's reign two centuries later.'

'I am honestly speechless,' said Genevieve at last, her hand on her forehead as she desperately processed everything that had just been disclosed to her. 'So we have kicked the proverbial catholic hornets' nest, and now we have a professional killer on our tail.'

'We need to see the stones at the memorial, get scans of them if possible, collate as much evidence as we can.' Said Cortez leaning forward picking up his backpack. Catherine and Anne nodded in unison, raising an arm gesturing in the direction of the grand French doors to the back of the room that led out onto the large patio area that then dropped to the expanse of the humongous lawns.

'Miss Silankis,' called Mrs Stirling apologetically as they were about to the leave through the patio doors. 'May I have a word with you in private?' Cortez left with Catherine and Anne as they trudged across the several acres of lawn towards the old memorial site. Once they were alone Mrs Stirling spoke, her soft voice sounding tired and thin.

'I must be honest with you Miss Silankis,' she started looking at her shoes and the highly polished parquet flooring. 'I have mentioned before of the financial difficulties that my family have been faced with. Our home was once filled with antiquities from all over the ancient world, monuments to rival the best museums and a library that would make any classical bibliophile jealous.'

Her pale, thin face blushed as she raised her tearful gaze to meet Genevieve's dark and beautiful eyes. 'Our family has once again fallen on hard times, as Dickens would say.

The cost of running the estate is over half a million pounds annually. Let alone my daughter's penchant for the lavish lifestyles and bravado of the heiresses they should be. To make ends meet I looked to auction off some of the pages...' she paused looking back at the table where they had just been sat where the velum pages still lay. 'Unfortunately, it brought unwanted attention to myself and my family from a nefarious man called Armon Di Silva, a black market arms dealer. He is a vile person, a prig, intent on growing his wealth no matter the cost or consequence. We tried to turn him away but his dogged determination and unscrupulous nature has sequentially passed that unwanted attention on to you. I am so sorry that this burden has ultimately fallen on you and resulted in you and your dear friend being hunted.'

Genevieve bit her lip, she was indignant but the desperation in the old lady's face calmed her instantly. Her annoyance would have to wait. She needed to gather information to formulate a plan, to save herself, Cortez and the Stirling family. 'We need to see those stones.' She called as she headed for the French doors.

*

Cafe Casa, London

Massimo sat silently in the beautiful morning sunshine outside of an independent Italian run upmarket coffee shop, his sunglasses covering his dark eyes, his face raised like a cold blooded lizard warming itself on a rock. He missed the warmth of home, southern Europe this time of year was easily fifteen degrees warmer than England. But he had a job to do, and as a professional you had to take the bad with the good.

His mobile phone vibrated on the café table as he allowed a lazy eye to see who was disturbing his morning ritual of proper coffee and a croissant. He half shrugged and let it go to voicemail.

He finished his heavily buttered and jam laden pastry before sucking each of his fingers clean, before wiping his mouth and hands with a scratchy paper napkin. He inhaled deeply, stretching out his strong shoulders as something behind him caught his eye. Pocketing his phone he slipped on his gloves before taking something from his plate he walked briskly to an alleyway a block away. He had seen the man following him, obviously an amateur as he made no attempt to hide the fact he was following him. Once he was around the corner and out of sight he stopped to check there were no cameras or vehicles parked nearby with Dash cameras.

He half turned to see the large man standing behind him, six four, two hundred pounds, transparent wire leading to an earpiece and a crisp blue cotton shirt with a stitched logo on the breast and clip on tie. 'Rent-a-cop' he muttered to himself.

'I need you to come with me Sir.' Asked the male authoritatively to the back of his target.

'You know I would love to but I have to go and fuck your mother right now,' replied Massimo with a shrug not turning around.

The security guard fired his Taser at Massimo's back as the two wired barbs sunk into his torso causing his spine to arch from the impact. The guard released the secondary charge as his face dropped. Massimo was somehow still standing.

The Italian turned slowly to face the guard, his eyes narrowed and sinister.

'Il mio turno… My turn.' Smiled Massimo. He leaped forward at lightning speed, grabbing the guard by his wrist twisting it sharply outwards at the same time he plunged the butter knife he had taken from the café table deep into the guards chest smearing the remnants of butter and jam from his morning coffee and croissant onto the crisp blue cotton uniform shirt.

The large man stood in utter shock as he looked down at the blunt lump of steel projecting from his chest. His face paled quickly as sweat appeared around his brow. Massimo pulled out the two barbs from his back with a wince, 'Cazzo..' he muttered to himself as he looked over his shoulder to assess the damage to his suit jacket.'You know how much this fucking jacket cost?' he swore.

The large guard's eyes were fixated on the knife still sticking out of his heaving chest. He placed a shaking hand on the bloodied handle but paused.

'You don't want to pull it out my friend, you will bleed out in fifteen seconds,' laughed the Italian lightly. 'Best leave it in,' he smiled maniacally.

'Who sent you?' asked Massimo, holding the man's cheeks roughly. The guard looked down at the gloves squeezing his face.

'I call it the Faraday Glove, after the maestro Michael Faraday,' started the Italian.

'Like his Faraday Cage, this glove and suit lining is made from a continuous covering of conductive material designed to block electromagnetic fields. But what makes this glove more spectacular is that I can harness up to 250,000 volts at my fingertips. And apply them wherever I deem fit.' He said placing his index finger onto the tip of the knife handle as the guard convulsed violently for less than two seconds as the steel blade piercing his heart released thousands of volts throughout his body. The large man fell to his knees making an animalistic groaning sound as foam and saliva dripped from his slack mouth.

'That was just a taster, so…' said Massimo, flicking the butt of the knife handle playfully. 'Who fucking sent you?'

*

Massimo closed the lid to the large red Biffa wheelie bin behind a questionable looking Chinese restaurant and relocked it before brushing himself down. Checking his voicemail he swore aloud as he listened.

'Signore Lupo, please be aware we have intercepted an alarming message, your client has issued a censure order on your services and is looking to end his contract.'

Massimo knew too well what a censure order meant for someone in his profession, death. It was what was issued when someone had messed up or taken too long on their contract. It was essentially a search and destroy request to ensure there were no traceable loose ends left.

He himself had concluded many of these orders but had never actually been the recipient of one. He dialled the number back, huffing indignantly.

'Che cazzo fei?' he roared tersely down the phone to his handler. 'Who do they think they are dealing with? Gino di fucking Campo?' He paused to see if his handler answered but the line was silent. 'What has happened?' he said seriously as he walked the busy streets. His dark eyes flitting around beneath his sunglasses checking every single member of the public within his peripheral vision. The deep voice finally replied,

'The contract has been placed on hold due to failure to stop the two targets meeting. You have put the client and the client's associates in immediate danger.'

'How long do I have?' he asked sincerely.

'Twenty-four hours,' came the blunt reply. 'You have until 0900hrs tomorrow. Failure is not an option. Be warned, other assets may be active.'

'Capito… I understand,' he replied calmly before hanging up. Checking his watch as it approached ten o'clock he dialled another number saved into his phone.

'Mike, Lima, Zero, Six, Alpha,' he said quietly. He waited for the beep then relayed his message. 'Single ticket, 0800hrs, tomorrow morning, Heathrow to Switzerland. ID sequence three.'

He hung up and cricked his neck. 'Always have an exit plan,' he sneered, his mind racing. 'Twenty-four hours…' he repeated to himself as he trudged away.

*

Stirling Mausoleum, Boreham House

The door to the mausoleum stood just over seven feet tall and six feet wide in the traditional arched triptych architecture of a church. The exterior walls were damp and crumbling and in need of serious repair, not to mention the years of ivy growth that hid the majority of damage beneath. Catherine removed a long heavy key from her jacket pocket and inserted it into the small lock beneath the large mottled brass handle. The door squeaked open but moved easily with no resistance. They all stepped inside as she hit a newly installed white plastic switch on the right hand side of the doorway. The room was immediately illuminated in a bright white light from three COB L.E.D bulbs fixed to the interior circular walls. The building smelt of old stone and damp similar to the room in St Peters.

Genevieve and Cortez made a bee-line for the ancient stones that stood all around three quarters of the building. Genevieve placed a hand on the first one, its hard surface was ice cold to the touch.

She looked at the circular hole a third of the way up, it had been filled from the other side with a rough mortar render mix. Although severely weathered the markings were still visible, she allowed her gentle fingers to caress the rutted contours of the ancient stone petroglyphs.

Her mind's-eye picturing the people ten thousand years ago chiselling them out with primitive stone tools. For a split second she was back in her dream, seeing the sun setting along the horizon directly above the row of standing stones, then the orange flame visible through the peephole.

'This is beautiful,' called Cortez loudly, abruptly bringing her back into the damp mausoleum as he wrestled his backpack off his hulking shoulders. 'This lighting is perfect for our scans, I will set up the tripod so we can do a 360 sweep.' He said as he began removing his equipment from his backpack.

Genevieve looked around at the series of small horizontal alcoves that sat between each of the large stones, each section had five alcoves and each one housed a stone urn. Beneath each urn was a brass plaque detailing whose remains lay within. Dozens of generations of the same family had been laid to rest within these hallowed walls, she looked over to Catherine and Anne and then to the last row of vertical alcoves that sat beside the large entrance. Four remained vacant, the top most occupied by a newer stone urn. The brass plaque had a man's name. 'Our father,' said Anne from behind her, following Genevieve's line of sight. 'He died ten years ago.'

'Skiing accident, supposedly,' said Catherine bitterly tapping the nearest standing stone.

Genevieve raised an eyebrow, 'Sorry… Supposedly?' she said almost apprehensively to Catherine.

'He was having an affair with some young ski instructor from Switzerland when they were both caught in an avalanche when off piste.' She turned to face the others. 'Mother is still in denial but we all know about it. No secrets in this household.'

'Catherine!' spat Anne indignantly as she closed in on her sister taking her by the arm. 'That is enough.'

Genevieve thought back to the house, of all the rooms they had seen, she hadn't seen a single photograph of Lord Stirling. This could explain why, the vindictive scorn of a betrayed wife. "I wonder if she destroyed them all" thought Genevieve subconsciously biting her cheek before she snapped back into the room.

'We will be the last Stirling's to be buried here.' said Catherine, pulling away from her sister's grip. She walked over to the four remaining alcoves looking at them despondently. 'Mother had radiotherapy back in the eighties, at some Harley Street pathology clinic. Unknowingly when she was pregnant with the two of us. Thanks to the doctor's lack of attention to detail we were both born sterile.' finished Catherine with a severe tone.

'I am so sorry.' replied Genevieve looking at the twin sisters. The obvious pain that came with infertility was evident in their eyes.

'So was mother.' spat Catherine.

'Right, all set.' smiled Cortez as he stepped back from the 3D scanner tripod arrangement he had built in the centre of the room. 'What did I miss?' he said looking around at the three female's melancholic body language.

*

'The scans are perfect. Just a shame we can't access the rear of the stones.' said Genevieve disappointedly, as she looked at the finished result via Cortez's laptop.

Cortez moved to the side of the centre most stone directly opposite the large entrance as he scratched away at the render with his thumb nail. 'This stuff is as solid as a rock.' He held back the temptation of singing it out in the pub style of Ashford and Simpson.

'There are recurring images,' started Genevieve as she tapped and screen shot certain images. 'If we can figure out what they mean we will be able to start figuring out the purpose of the stones.'

As she stood up to join Cortez they were interrupted by the sound of approaching footsteps, they were heavy and in quick succession. Cortez placed his hand into his backpack as he stepped in front of Genevieve shielding her front the main entrance. His traditional approach to chivalry made her feel warm inside.

The weighty footsteps belonged to one of the houses security team, one that Cortez and Genevieve hadn't seen before.

The tall rotund suited female had her blonde hair tied back in an insanely tight bun similar to an airline steward, her hand was fixed to her underarm beneath her suit jacket.

As she ran inside her eyes scanned left to right checking both Catherine and Anne were all in order, then radioed through a hidden microphone somewhere in her jacket sleeve. 'Bringing the chicks in now.' she spat as her barrelled chest heaved heavily. She swooped her arms around the Stirling twins and marched them out of the mausoleum.

'What is going on?' asked Cortez as he threw his equipment into his backpack. 'Is there a problem?'

The security guard didn't even look back as she spoke, 'The gatehouse has called in an abandoned vehicle to the south of the perimeter wall. No driver and the passenger window has been smashed.' Genevieve and Cortez exchanged a worried look and ran after them towards the main house.

As they approached the French doors three more security guards filed out to meet them. Their eyes off to the horizon scanning the large expanse of the open lawns. Unlike their drivers and the female escorting them back to the house, these three security guards carried G36 assault rifles and wore thick Kevlar vests.

Once everyone was inside the doors were secured and they were all escorted upstairs into a large library study with small sashed windows along one wall. Thick wooden shutters were placed over the three windows and the double doors were locked, an armed guard on either side.

One of the guards whispered into his sleeve then turned to Mrs Stirling, a severe stare on his face. 'Once we have conducted a full sweep of the grounds and house we can relax a bit. But for now we need you all to stay in this room.' He moved over to the other three armed guards inside the sealed room whispering to them as they nodded and looked over to Cortez and Genevieve.

'I don't like this Genny.' Muttered Cortez as he eyeballed the armed guards.

*

Chapter 6
Battle at Boreham House

Camden Town, London

Massimo ambled casually into a deserted multi-storey car park beside a large supermarket and walked several rows until he stopped in front of an old Ford Mondeo. Looking through the passenger window he could see a pile of old receipts and several empty sweet packets, 'Promising'. His eyes glanced to the dash where a dark LED poked up from the dust covered mottled plastic. No signs of life, 'Perfetto' he smiled. Tapping the car window with his elbow no alarm sounded. So he struck again with all his force shattering the windows glass into a tight spider web before it fell inwards in a thousand tiny pieces. He lent through the window and unlocked the door which released the opposite driver's door. Slunking into the driver's seat he quickly opened the glove box to see what the owner had left inside. The messy and unkempt state of the car's interior was a clear sign that the owner was lazy and gave absolutely no regard to the car, and was unlikely to spend money fixing the faulty alarm. As he rummaged through he found several unopened letters, more empty sweets packets and a thin leather folder. He pulled out the latter and opened it to find the vehicles log book, two historic mot certificates and a spare car key attached to a small plastic garage key fob. His smile grew as he slid the key into the ignition and turned as the old Ford growled into life. 'Got to love lazy people' he said to no one.

His drive was uneventful and smooth, on seeing the high wall running the entire perimeter of the house he pulled up along the empty picturesque rural lane.

Dumping the car on the opposite verge he left the key in the ignition and began his walk along the high wall. He found a section of the wall he was looking for, the wall was dilapidated with several stones missing and the verge rose up by several feet making the overall height that bit lower. He stood in the road and eyed it before taking a quick dash up the verge, jumping up and grabbing the top of the stone wall using the missing stones as foot holds. He slid over the top effortlessly and disappeared on to the other side.

Moving from tree line to tree line he sprinted up the lawns towards the large house some several hundred metres away. Pausing to assess the layout and extent of the security detail he took out a monocular sweeping from side to side. He could see lots of security cameras, random patrols of several suited guards walking the grounds, no signs of any dog units which he was glad to see. And, he smiled again, the French doors to the rear of the house were sitting wide open.

Checking the best route he could see a low trench dug into the manicured grounds that served as drainage from the raised lawn above. This led to a stepped area that fed to the base of the large patio area outside the rear of the house. Watching the suited guards walk past him on three occasions completely unaware that he was so close to them he crept closer and closer to the main house. On reaching the patio and beside the French door he could hear a commotion from inside then the sound of hefty footsteps. Throwing himself against the wall he watched as a large blonde female ran out of the house and off towards an old building half a mile away. Slipping inside he started phase two of his plan.

The house was silent other than several large grandfather clocks tick-tocking away to themselves. The Italian became almost invisible as he stealthily moved around the house counting security personnel, exit routes and family members. Thus far he counted four downstairs, three upstairs and the primary target Stirling Senior. He watched as three of the guards began donning Kevlar vests removing G36 assault rifles from a secure Chippendale cabinet as they headed for the patio area. Two men escorted Stirling senior upstairs so he followed suit. From his previous reconnaissance of the upstairs, he knew she had been taken into the library. He also knew that there was a conjoining bathroom that could be accessed from a separate bedroom so this was where he headed.

Concealed in the bathroom he listened at the library door as several others joined the original three. With his ear pressed against the pine door he could make out what was being said, 'Once we have conducted a full sweep of the grounds and house we can relax a bit. But for now we need you all to stay in this room.'

At the sound of arguing Massimo removed his Sig Sauer P320 and screwed on the custom suppressor. Something didn't sound right and this intrigued him greatly.

*

Stirling Residence, Boreham House

Cortez felt an uneasy turn in his stomach, the type of feeling you get when things are about to go sideways. He had a complicated history of violence long before he had become the head of security at the Old Vic Theatre. The last time he got this feeling things had turned bad for everyone. He silently placed his hand back into his open backpack as he watched the armed security team begin to squabble amongst themselves. Two of them were acting strangely, not calm and collected like the others. As more of the security team entered the room he signalled subtly to Genevieve looking towards the adjoining door away from the security team. Standing off to the right of the pine door he sat her down and leant in close whispering into her ear as Mrs Stirling, Catherine and Anne stood talking beside the ornate wooden writing desk.

Mrs Stirling brought out a silver Samsonite case and placed it on the table next to Genevieve as Cortez eyed up the squabbling security team. Opening the case they could see that it contained two small pages each housed inside a Perspex case. These pages, unlike the Lindisfarne Gospels Genevieve had examined the day before, were much older and of very different design and structure.

'Although a recent addition, these are one of my family's most prized possessions.' Said Mrs Stirling proudly. 'These are segments cut from the same scroll.'

'Scroll?' questioned Genevieve excitedly, coming to stand beside her.

'Yes, they date to 45 AD, written by the Roman surveyor Antonius Pietra.' replied Mrs Stirling.

Her daughter spoke as they gathered around. 'They refer to the pagan tribes of Iron Age Britain, especially the Trinovantes of Colchester and St Albans. It mentions a local man called Cintusmus who acted as a guide to the Roman invading forces. Cintusmus related all the local knowledge, history, myth and legend and took the surveyors to all the significant ritualistic sites of the area.'

The pages were of a thick ancient paper and consisted of dozens of lines written by stylus. The grey ink print was either tar or octopus ink, each letter was small and concise and very neatly scribed.

'This text details the location of the standing stones, its path and the alignment across southern Britannia. The second text details the use of the stones.'

'A moment if you please Mrs Stirling,' interrupted Cortez, taking her arm he leant in close and lowered his voice to an almost whisper. 'The security team appears to be a little… Anxious. Is everything in order?'

Nicola turned to watch as the gathered security personnel became visibly agitated towards each other. 'We have a safe room to the side of that fireplace.' she replied using her eyes to point out the location to Cortez.

Cortez watched as the eight armed security team continued to bicker and quibble behind them. 'When we create a distraction, get your daughters inside the safe room and do not open it until we call you.' He turned to look her in the eye, 'Do you understand?' Mrs Stirling nodded and moved back over to be with her daughters.

'Genny, don't react but I don't like the look of how this is progressing.' He paused waiting for his words to sink in. Genevieve nodded gently and squeezed his hand. 'Ok,' he continued. 'When I say so, make an excuse to leave, ask to use the loo or something. Be adamant that you need to go through that door behind you. I need to get you and the Stirling's to a place of safety.'

He brushed her wild hair behind her ear and ran his thumb down her cheek. 'Be careful.' He stood back and walked over to the Stirling's.

'I need to spend a penny,' called Genevieve aloud, making everyone stop talking and look her way. 'Is it through here?' she asked as she tried to open the pine door nearest to them and furthest away from the gathered security team.

'Don't open that door!' called one of the armed security guards. 'Not until we have successfully searched the entire house and grounds.'

Cortez moved across the room in several large strides coming to stand behind the Stirling family. Leaning in he whispered when close enough for them to hear him.

'Is this part of your security lockdown procedure?' He eyed Mrs Stirling intensely. She nodded gently in reply, but her eyes flitted to the two guards arguing with the rest of the security team. Cortez followed her eyes to watch them for a second, then continued, 'Do you recognise all of these people?' his tone was serious, 'Is there anyone in this room you haven't seen before?'

Mrs Stirling swallowed then answered, her voice croaky and thin, 'All but those two. I have not seen them before. I fear this is what they are arguing about.'

'I am sorry but I really need to go,' spat Genevieve loudly from the other side of the room. Cortez pushed Anne, Catherine and Nicola towards the fireplace ushering them to the entrance of their safe room, 'Open it and get inside, quickly.'

Genevieve pushed open the pine door to enter the large Jack and Jill bathroom. She froze on the spot on seeing Massimo standing silently behind the door, she moved to scream for Cortez to help but Massimo silenced her, before she knew it his rough fingers were cupped around her mouth and his pistol raised.

'Silenzio Principessa.' he whispered silkily into her ear. She wriggled in disgust as she tried to free herself from his grasp.

From the other room the squabbling security team broke form as one of the unknown guards pushed the other as the second imposter removed their knife before impaling it hilt deep into one of the regular security team member's neck.

Four more members of the security team appeared at the door, assault rifles raised, ready.

'Who the fuck are you?' shouted another of the regular security team. He turned back to see his colleague had been stabbed in the neck. 'Right!' he spat, raising his own rifle.

All this happened in an instant and the infighting escalated quickly before shots were fired. Cortez burst through the bathroom door as the shooting started, he landed heavily on his back after jumping the last several metres. The Samsonite case firmly in his hand. Massimo looked down at him but simply stepped over him, poking his head around the door frame taking out three of the hostile security team. The hollow "*thut, thut, thut*" still caused an echo within the bathroom.

'This is my contract mother fuckers!' he shouted indignantly as he again fired around the door frame.

The remaining security guards reciprocated by releasing a volley towards the bathroom door. As they returned fire Mrs Stirling had successfully secured her family into their hidden safe room beside the fireplace. Massimo and the remaining security team continued to battle it out. By now the two hostile security guards and the remaining regular team had taken defensive positions now crouching behind the solid furniture and stone plinths around the library. Shooting both at each other and back across to the bathroom.

In all the confusion Genevieve & Cortez made for the grand staircase, Cortez checked all the corridors and main stairwell before he ushered Genevieve under his large arm.

'Keep moving Genny!' he called affirmatively as he led the way. Their progress was quick and they met little resistance, until they came to the last corridor before the lower stairwell. 'Wait here!' he shouted as he pushed Genevieve back into a recess with a reassuring little nod before he disappeared around the corner. She heard a loud grunt, a faint thud and a sickening click and cracking sound before he returned beside her. 'Come on, keep moving.' He ordered.

As she rounded the corner she could see one of the imposter security team lying spread eagle on the floor, their neck twisted to the side at an unhealthy angle. She paused at the sight, 'Genny, look at me.' called Cortez, placing his large hands either side of her small face, diverting her gaze to him, 'Keep looking at me, not them, ok?' he said again rubbing his thumb against her pale cheek. 'Looking at me, yeah.'

They bounded down the stairs and off to the side away from the front door where they had entered as more security officers charged inside, guns raised, some shouting into their sleeves, others pressing their ear comms to hear their colleagues cries from upstairs.

Cortez led them through to an expansive and luxurious kitchen and out into a huge car garage attached to the side of the extensive manor. They could see half a dozen very nice cars parked in a neat row along the rear wall. Cortez ran over to the secure wall mounted cabinet beside the fancy tool bank and opened it to reveal several sets of keys on small hooks. He spun around to take in what options he had.

Orange Jeep 4x4, Black Porsche, Silver Lexus, Cream Tesla, Dark Blue Mercedes and the Armoured Range Rover Evoque they had arrived in. His first instinct was the armoured vehicle, but the key was missing. "Fuck!" he spat internally. 'We need to be silent,' he thought aloud, picking up the Tesla key.

Cortez floored the *borrowed* Tesla, its wide wheels kicking up the white gravel and dust from the pristine driveway as it skidded away up the winding drive. It looked impressive as its wheels spun away but the entire movement was ghostly silent with only the tip tapping of falling gravel making a sound.

'We have to get to the research offices at the University lab to check these texts.' Shouted Cortez, his ears still ringing from the gunfire.

Genevieve was too busy trying her mobile telephone, 'It won't connect.' She snapped as she kept trying Mrs Stirling's mobile. Her hands were shaking uncontrollably.

'We have another problem…' snapped Cortez looking up ahead to the main gate house. 'It looks like Mrs Stirling has hired a private army.'

Seven security officers stood in a line blocking the exit gate, their semi-automatic rifles raised and trained on their approaching Tesla. Cortez took immediate evasive action and swerved hard to his left, going off road over the bumpy grass following the high metal fence until it became the old stone boundary wall.

Cortez kept the vehicle over ninety miles per hour, checking his mirror he could see they did not pursue them on foot.

The Tesla continued its course around the perimeter of the manor's grounds, it bounced silently over the rough grassy terrain as Cortez continued around the track.

'There is no gap in the wall, we may need to try the main gate again.' he said despondently. 'We are about a quarter way round the estate-' he paused at seeing a sole male running at full sprint away from the manor. It was *The Wolf*. He was being chased by three large Alsatian dogs, fast dogs. They watched him disappear over the bank that dropped to a lower area of the grounds, the dogs did not jump after him but stood and barked menacingly after him.

Further round the wall Genevieve noticed a smaller gate opening in the boundary wall. 'There!' she called pointing to their right as the gate opened onto a wooded lane.

Swinging the car through the open gate Cortez slowed down as they entered the dense woodland. The tall trees created a canopy over the mud path casting the vehicle interior into shadow.

They stopped outside a small free standing stone building, outside it sat a small four wheeled buggy and a large maintenance truck. On the other side of the road sat several orange traffic cones topped off with red and white tap cordoning off an area of broken wall, beside the cones sat half a dozen piles of the dry wall stones stacked up resembling cairns.

After reversing the Tesla back out of the way Cortez turned to Genevieve, her face now completely white, her hands still shaking uncontrollably. 'Stay here!' he called as he jumped out and headed for the large maintenance truck. No keys in the ignition but he had hardly expected there to be any. He slipped open the tool box, sat on the passenger seat and removed the flat head screwdriver and the Stanley knife. Within seconds he had removed the plastic casing underneath the steering wheel and was cutting at several wires with the Stanley knife. The diesel engine kicked into life and he sat upright in the driver's seat. He pushed the door wide open with his foot then slipped the truck into first gear. The truck trundled towards the partially damaged stone wall as he manhandled the vehicle through the gears, collecting momentum quickly.

Cortez held fast, his arms keeping the wheel straight until he was ten feet away from the crumbling wall, he glanced back to Genevieve, he knew he had to get her out of this situation. Five feet away he jumped out of the truck, his landing was surprisingly agile for a man of his large build. The truck ploughed through the old wall sending moss covered stone fragments out in every direction amid a dense cloud of pale dust before it rolled to a slow stop in the adjacent field. Cortez walked up to the now gaping wall kicking one or two remaining stones out of the way he brushed himself down and walked back to the Tesla.

'Shall we?' he smiled reassuringly, but it was hopeless she was too deep in shock. He pushed the ignition button as they drove silently through the new hole and turned off back onto the small road away from the Manor and the grounds.

*

Massimo reached the small opening in the boundary wall that he had used to access the grounds. He bounded up the internal side of the wall and poked his head over the top, all was clear. He sideways rolled over the top and landed stealthily, bending his knees as he landed. He turned and swore again. After everything he had just been through this was the final straw, his stolen car was gone, 'Fucking car thieves.' he spat indignantly, wiping the sweat from his brow as he began to jog down the road.

Two miles down the road he came to a small electrical substation that branched off from the road. He could see the small wire gate was open and the lights on inside. Outside sat a light blue Vespa with an open faced helmet perched on the seat. Looking back up the road he finally gave a wry smile. 'Perfetto.'

A startled engineer came bounding out of the sub-station as Massimo raced off up the road on his Vespa. Massimo removed his mobile sending a text with his left hand as his right held the throttle back to its maximum. This reminded him of his youth, his teenage years spent roaming the narrow streets of Italy on his own Vespa. Trying his hardest to fit in with the humble locals, only to be found out, they taunted him with the mocking phrase, *figlio di papà*, abused and slapped when they found out the truth of his lies regarding his privileged heritage.

It was hard to hide the fact that your mother was a Countess from one of Italy's oldest noble families. His younger years had been lonely, the isolation overwhelmingly tough for one so young.

His parents were always socialising, holidaying or *"on business trips"* as they would tell him. Their absence in his childhood meant leaving him in the hands and at the mercy of his strict tutor and nanny, Sister Margarette. He shuddered at the memory as he rode through the lush green countryside.

The tranquillity of the quiet country lane was disrupted by the 2-stroke pop-pop of the Vespa's engine. His mind took him back to those times, secluded in their huge mansion on Lago Como.

Sister Margarette was an ancient thug of a woman, at two metres tall and well into her eighties the Catholic Nun looked more like a retired American Footballer in bad drag than a saintly vestal. She encouraged traditional and cruel methods of education. She believed in hard discipline and absolute obedience, two things that little Massimo had always challenged. His reward for his natural curiosity and innocent cheek, a long stiff cane on the backside and clips round the ears. He had despised the woman and all that she stood for. He had imagined many scenes in his mind of how she would accidentally fall down the stairs or choke on one of her cannoli's, the small Italian sweet snack she adamantly refused to share with Massimo.

Then on his thirteenth birthday without so much as a *"buon compleanno"* she had raised her arm to strike him but instead of wincing and taking it he had blocked it. That was the day she was found at the bottom of the marble staircase of the family mansion. The paramedics had concluded the elderly sister had stumbled on her habit and fallen to her death in a tragic accident.

The only person who knew the truth was Massimo. That day, his thirteenth birthday he had become the man he was today, cold, calculated and emotionally dead inside. The textbook sociopath. His parents took to hiring a younger tutor, this time one not connected to the church. Massimo had learnt very quickly that he could use his family's wealth to his own benefit, in that he would handsomely bribe the new naive tutor to tell his parents that he was studying as expected, but he would go off to find children to socialise with. But the psychological changes in him had made it hard for him to play and engage with, and fit in with the local children wherever he moved from one small town to the next looking for someone to call his friend, and he moved around a lot. He tried to forget his past and create a new life, but whatever he did they always ended up finding out his true nature and background. No matter where he went the children always taunted him with the same phrase, *figlio di papà*.

It was only when he became an adult, joining the fierce 9th Paratroopers Assault Regiment that he felt welcomed and amongst his own like-minded people. He excelled in every aspect of the unit ethos, his professional career and development like no others. He was finally home.

Massimo looked up from his mobile and swerved violently as a huge green and yellow John Deere Tractor sat blocking the entire carriageway, 'Cazzo!' He rose up onto the verge and continued his journey, putting the phone away giving the road his utmost attention. He was nearing his destination, the University of Essex Colchester Campus. But first he needed to change his clothes and collect a few necessary pieces of equipment.

*

Essex Police Headquarters, Chelmsford

'Are you sure about this?' she asked him hesitantly as Genevieve and Cortez drove into the visitor's car park of the Essex Police building.

'Trust me, with what we just saw, we need to let the professionals take the lead.' replied Cortez. 'Besides, the shit we've been through today, I think we could both do with the rest. And there ain't much place safer than this.'

They climbed out and walked into the front counter. The raised desk was occupied by two people in uniform and a security door positioned on either side one said "Custody" the other "Authorised Personnel Only". The closest of them greeted them with a smile and raised eyebrows.

'Is DI Thorgood in?' asked Cortez, brightly tapping his fingers on the raised desk.

'Detective Inspector Thorgood…' replied the desk officer correctively looking him up and down, 'One minute.' as he picked up the phone.

A large attractive woman in a sharp suit appeared at the security door beside the front counter, her thick Scottish accent boomed around the small entrance room. 'Cortez you ugly wee basterd, what brings you in here.'

They embraced and she threw Genevieve a sideways look, 'And who is this wee angel?'

Cortez made the introduction then gave a serious look, 'We need to talk.'

Minutes later they were sitting inside her office amidst the throng of the CID offices on the second floor. Manilla folders were stacked high on every work surface blocking in ancient computer screens with aged curling Post-It notes with *"BROKEN I.T. AWARE"* written on them. Coffee-stained floor tiles and broken office chairs littered the floors. Several officers sat typing away or burying their heads in their hands as they read through case files.

The large lady shut the office door and turned to sit opposite them. 'So, by the look on your face this ain't a social call Cortez. What brings you to see old Sally Thorgood then?' she started. 'Mind if I vape?' she added as she sucked on a small metal cylinder releasing a strawberry scented cloud into the room.

Cortez and Genevieve relayed everything they had uncovered and all that had transpired over the past two days. DI Thorgood sat in silence as she took it in, she leant in closer when they mentioned The Wolf. 'Why the feck didya not go straight to the MET? A professional fucking hitman with a firearm walking around capping people!'

They continued their debrief up until that moment, she puffed on her vape but otherwise she said nothing and made no intention to write anything down. When they had finally finished she stood up and walked over to the window looking out at the busy roundabout across the road.

'Well this is not what I was expecting, Cortez. Thank you for coming in here and dumping this shite on my desk.' She turned around with a serious look. 'This is major crimes stuff, not plain CID. I am going to have to take this upstairs, figuratively speaking. Christ, they will ask all sorts of pain in the arse questions.' She inhaled heavily on the vaper and expelled a large cloud of strawberry smoke. 'You carrying?' she asked Cortez, still staring out of the office window. Cortez shook his fuzzy, hairy head.

'You know I don't like guns, Sal.' he replied, she just scoffed as she banged on the window at someone outside. 'Aye' she muttered.

'Hm... I've half a mind to ask you two to leave.' the large Scot continued, raising a knowing eyebrow. 'We could pretend you never came in here and you take this back for the Metropolitan police to investigate.'

'Sally, come on,' started Cortez leaning forward in desperation. 'I would feel better knowing that we had you on our side with this one. You know what could happen.' he paused, a look of guilt flittered into his eyes. 'You owe me one.' he said earnestly.

She looked at him sternly then broke her gaze, 'Och fine...' she huffed. She turned her monitor around 180 degrees and slid her keyboard over to him. 'Type it up and I will start the ball rolling.'

'Thank you Sally, you are the best.' replied Cortez happily as he began tapping away on the keyboard.

'Aye, I am the best. Don't you forget it.' She said looking down at her vape. 'Och, screw this I am going out for a real fag. Be done and gone by the time I get back up here.' she said hotly, taking a packet of cigarettes from her top draw as she walked out of the room.

Within minutes Cortez had completed the lengthy statement. He stood up and scribbled a note leaving it on DI Thorgood's desk as he turned to leave. They walked out of the Police headquarters using the main door. It was bustling with people, the noise and chaos was somewhat soothing to them.

Genevieve climbed back into the passenger seat and clipped in her seat belt before she turned to Cortez and asked, 'How do you know her? The DI?'

Cortez half smiled and explained, 'We served together in the Special Forces, years ago. I moved up from Army to Special Forces, that is where I met her. She was the only woman on the squad. Back then it was tougher for them, there were a lot of idiots in the forces back then. People that didn't like the idea of women serving and fighting for the crown.' Cortez started the car and pulled away slowly, 'Sally was, *is* tough.' he corrected himself. 'She never let those oppressors win. Never let them get one over her, no matter what they threw at her she held her chin high and proud.' He paused for a moment as though reliving a scene in his mind. 'Then one day our CO, commanding officer went too far. He ordered her to strip to her briefs and undergo a Beasting from some of our seniors along with the rest of us.'

'What is a Beasting?' she asked quizzically.

'Your unit *jumps* on you when you least expect it and they give you a good kicking. Most of the time it is a playful bundle with a few cheap shots. It was designed to toughen us up, but this was a targeted and malicious attack. Some of the senior officers had harassed her for years, made false allegations, and doctored her performance and psychological stats.' He visibly gripped the steering wheel as he spoke, his knuckles whitening.

'What happened?' she asked apprehensively.

'After we gave her a few smacks the senior officers ordered us all out of the barracks. They stayed in there with her. Those fuckers carried on and they nearly killed her.'

Genevieve grabbed her mouth in shock. 'Oh my goodness, that is terrible.'

Cortez nodded solemnly, 'That wasn't all they did. Those animals tried to rape her whilst she lay semi-conscious on the barrack floor, covered in her own blood and half naked. One of them was a bloody Army Chaplain.'

'I can't believe this.' cried Genevieve, feeling cold inside from what Cortez had just told her.

'Well I couldn't let them do this to one of our own, she had saved my life more than once when on the battlefield and I hers… So I went back in there.' said Cortez quietly.

'And I got her out of there. You can imagine how it went from there and that five senior officers don't take kindly to having their jaws broken and arms snapped by an NCO. I was dishonourably discharged the same day, we both were.'

'What about the officers? What happened to the five suspects?' she asked uncomfortably.

'There is a very dark side to the British Military, always has been. There are a lot of cover ups and red tape when it comes to army clergy, malevolent officers or unintentional cockups resulting in deaths. You would be ashamed at the number of historical incidents labelled as suicides.' he paused. 'Sorry, this is all a bit heavy.' He coughed awkwardly and remained silent for a few minutes as he drove.

'All five officers were questioned but never faced any official charges and no hearing was ever undertaken by the MP, military police. We were ordered to sign an OSA order, official secrets act that silenced us from speaking out about what had actually happened. Sally later joined the police rising to Detective Inspector, I started my private security company and ran most of the entertainment venues security in Greater London and Essex. We help each other out every now and then. She is one of the people that I trust with my life.'

'When we were in her office earlier, you told her she owed you…' started Genevieve, 'You weren't referring to what happened back then were you?'

'Goodness no, Genny!' spat Cortez. 'What do you take me for,' he shook his head indignantly. 'We agreed never to mention the incident again after it happened.' He muttered to himself before continuing, 'When I said you owe me one. That was a few months ago when I helped her hack…' he cut himself off, 'I mean I aided her in accessing a few servers belonging to one of her suspects for a case she was working on. She had reached a dead end and needed my help.'

'What if she needs more information about all of this?' she asked, tapping the Samsonite case on her lap.

'Everything is in the report.' he replied with a smile. 'Here we are.' he said as they pulled into the University of Essex Colchester Campus. 'Let's check out those texts, come on dove.'

*

Undisclosed Location

Ordo Solis Secret Meeting Conclave Chamber for the Catholic Church

'The Italians are obsessed with the British Monarchy.' laughed an old man in a red Cardinal robe and red galero hat. In his mid sixties the man had a stern face and harsh eyes. His face and scalp were clean shaven, revealing a small reddish brown birthmark behind his left ear.

He wore small round framed glasses pinched at the tip of his large nose. 'I would wager that if you had an Englishman and an Italian side by side, the Italian would be able to answer more questions about the Royals,' The man paused as someone across the room coughed loudly and indignantly. The universal sound made to silence a bustling room.

'Gentlemen,' called another elderly male dressed in a matching red robe and galero. 'This council has been gathered to discuss the situation in England.' The room was filled with thirty of the most senior Cardinals from the Sacred College of Cardinals. Those selected out of the 203 active cardinals from 69 countries, these thirty men were the ones with all the power, the ones that actually selected the successor for the role of Pope. 'The threat to our establishment and fraternity is very real. The escalation is getting way out of hand and without the necessary management we are looking at global incidents and total exposure.' The room of Cardinals began muttering disdainfully. 'Domenico,' snapped the old man, 'What progress have you made?'

The entire room of Cardinals turned to face the birthmarked man, Domenico, the ensembled chamber was deathly silent.

'The Inspector of Ancient Monuments has been silenced,' replied the old birthmarked man sardonically, as a repost to the other Cardinals comment. 'And we are in the process of acquiring all documentation and eliminating all that knows of the Goddess Path.' The room erupted in a fervour of angered rumblings as the congregated males started making the sign of the cross. 'We have a team working on it as we speak.' He glanced across to the man beside him.

'You had better have this under control by the end of today, Domenico.' replied the lead Cardinal. 'Now to other business.' He continued to address the room.

Domenico sniffed indignantly as he muttered to the man beside him, 'I should have taken your advice,' he paused looking around him, 'Not to work with that idiot arms dealer Armon Di Silva.'

The other man remained silent, 'Hmm.' he raised an eyebrow knowingly as if to test him.

'We will have to clean this mess up ourselves.' continued Domenico, 'I assembled a team to go to England as you asked, they are at Boreham House as we speak.'

They both made the sign of the cross, head, chest, shoulder to shoulder. The old man took out his mobile phone as he received a text message, <*From: Signore Lupo, Your team failed. They are all dead. I am following the target and documents now. Call off your hounds. Lupo*>

'Cazzo.' spat the birthmarked man, mopping his sweating head, he stood to leave the room as the lead cardinal grabbed him hard by the arm. 'Do not fail.' he said in an imposing voice. His dark eyes were unfaltering. Domenico remained silent, placing his phone back inside his robes, he nodded stupidly back at the senior cardinal.

'In eius luce et gratia.' they muttered as one.

*

Chapter 7
Campus Chaos

University of Essex Colchester Campus

Cortez had called ahead, arranging to be met by one of the leading forensic scientists at the University. Both sections of the scroll were scanned and fragments taken for chemical analysis and isotope analysis.

'The problem with these old texts is that they are so hard to authenticate and date.' smiled Beth, the lab assistant. 'We can run an analysis on the more common inks used but we can only compare them to those we have in our collection. We have more from the 7th century onwards, but we can try and get an accurate date as they used the same techniques for decades. But these old Roman texts… It is very hard to date the ink as some bottles were used for decades and the technique has not changed for nearly 500 years.'

They looked into a set of high definition microscope lenses that showed an extremely close up display of the text held beneath. The colours of the grey ink now a mixture of purple and yellow and black lines, even the miniscule brush strokes of the stylus were now visible.

'It will take about three hours for the results to come through,' smiled the young lab scientist.

'Can we get it translated as well?' asked Cortez looking over the assistant's shoulder.

'Already on it,' she replied, tapping another screen displaying a red box with "*ANALYSING*" written above a small buffering circle. The red box pinged green as the word changed to "*COMPLETE*".

The lab assistant clicked a button and the translated transcript began printing from behind them.

'We can call you when the ink isotope analysis is completed.' she smiled, handing over the print out to Cortez.

'Lunch?' beamed Cortez, rolling up the translation into a slim tube in his large hands.

He escorted Genevieve through the maze of the University grounds until they reached the food hall. It was full of people of all ages, some young, mostly middle aged and then there were those mature students that looked as though they should have retired years ago.

He carried their laden tray to an empty table and handed over a white Styrofoam carton containing a steaming jacket potato with all the trimmings. He opened their plastic coffee cups and poured in several sugars before giving them a stir. 'Strong and black Genny, here you go.' He passed her steaming cup over as he unwrapped his sandwich taking a huge bite, chewing greedily. The morning's exertions having taken its toll on his energy levels.

'Genny,' he started earnestly taking her hand as she stared almost comatose at her potato. 'Let me address the elephant in the room.' he started. She looked around her but seemed lost. He continued, giving her hand a gentle squeeze. 'About what I had to do back at the manor…' He looked into her reddened eyes and paused. He huffed trying to find the right words. He always found it so hard to tell someone he cared so much about how he found it so easy to *dispose* of a living human being and still have an appetite. 'That man that I took out, they would have killed us if I hadn't taken action. I just hope you understand that I didn't enjoy any of it… I only did what I had to. To protect you.' He looked around at the young faces sitting around them, all so innocent, so carefree and no skeletons in their closet.

Genevieve nodded silently, she smiled softly and bit her lip. 'Thank you.' she replied softly. She took a deep swig of her coffee and closed her eyes, her head had been throbbing all afternoon. 'Let's put it behind us and focus on something else.' She reached for the print out on the paper roll and unfurled it.

The text was displayed in two row segments down the page, the top read as the original Roman text, the line below was the translation. They leant in close to read it together, Genevieve finishing before Cortez. She closed her eyes, her mind racing. Cortez slumped back in his chair and exhaled loudly.

'So this confirms it then.' he smiled, 'The stone paths were a ritualistic transition for adolescent females from childhood into adulthood. A method of gleaning all that was needed to create and sustain life itself. Each stone path route teaches them recognition and awareness of dangers, comprehension of life skills, and the passing on of all knowledge.'

'The path of the Goddess.' said Genevieve. 'We need to find Flint, find out where he got all his information from. See if he can clarify how Edward the Confessor used this against the Church.'

'I will put the word out that we are looking for him, see if he bites.' said Cortez taking his phone out.

Genevieve's mobile rang as she held it up on speaker for them both to hear,

'Hello Ms Silankis. It's Beth from the lab. The results are back – certified 30-110 AD. Looks like your scroll is legitimate.' came the young voice. 'We have something to show you.'

They entered the lab carrying their Styrofoam cups, to find it was now empty. The positioning of the documents and equipment looked as though the staff were mid-research when they had left. Cortez took up a position in the doorway as he checked the corridor feeling uneasy once again. Genevieve checked her mobile but it had no service signal.

'This doesn't feel right Genny.' called Cortez from the doorway. He walked back towards her checking the lab for a weapon. Other than monitors, cables and high specification computer equipment there was nothing he could use. He turned on the spot raising his arms like a boxer as the young lab technician appeared through the door with a broad smile carrying a couple of ceramic mugs. She paused in shock at Cortez's behaviour, but smiled awkwardly at them as she carried the drinks inside.

'Sorry for being a bit intense, we've had a bit of a crazy day.' smiled Cortez with a shrug, lowering his large arms.

The young lady nodded as she pointed over to the monitor, she relayed what she had found and read through the results. Half an hour passed when Cortez's mobile phone pinged, a text message from his old friend DI Thorgood <*Heads up big man, stolen vespa from near to Stirling house seen travelling towards the Uni. x*>

'We need some sort of protection,' snapped Cortez, placing the phone back into his pocket. 'Can you contact campus security and ask them to be on the look out for an Italian male, mid 30's, well dressed, riding a Vespa.'

The forensic scientist just looked at him coyly. 'The security here probably won't help you much. Plus, we have about 200 Italian students on site matching that description.'

Cortez just huffed deeply. 'There a workshop in this University?' he smiled back at Beth.

'There is a tool box in the cupboard.' replied the lab technician sheepishly pointing to the tall row of cupboards beside them. Cortez searched high and low before turning back to face them with a broad smile on his hairy face, his large hands wrapped around a hefty iron crowbar.

*

The skyline was glistening with lights from the thousands of houses along the horizon, the dark evening sky was clear and full of stars. Cortez was tapping away on the research lab's main computer when he huffed loudly, 'Not again!' He slammed his hands down in frustration and pushed the chair back with his bottom. Standing up he muttered more to himself, 'I will check the servers, you wait here. And keep the door locked.' said Cortez walking off, shouldering the large crowbar as he whistled "Whistle While You Work" jauntily.

Genevieve continued to read the old manuscripts laid out on the tables, her back to the office door. She heard a noise behind her and began speaking aloud, 'Beth, we need to check on the-' Genevieve turned and dropped her coffee cup, sending the rich black liquid rushing to the marble floor, it shattered instantly as her black coffee exploded like a Jackson Pollock painting by her feet.
From within the shadows of the room came a figure, a figure holding a large revolver in their right hand.

'You must be Armon Di Silva.' said Genevieve flatly, swallowing hard, willing her racing heart to slow down.
The large man nodded but remained silent. His dark eyes flared intently as he looked Genevieve up and down. His menacing glare made her feel uneasy.
'We have what you want, it is in that case…' She spoke softly, her shaking hand pointing towards the silver samsonite suitcase lying on the opposite side of the room. The large man's sinister eyes flickered quickly over to it but he continued to stare at her as his face erupted into a broad smile. He appeared to be toying with her.
He stepped forward causing Genevieve to retreat backward, her thigh hitting the table behind her. Her cheeks reddened at her mistake.

'Bring it to me.' he ordered in a low husky voice. His accent was a mixture of harsh Portuguese and rough English and one of a perpetual smoker. He held out his left hand ushering her to fetch the case for him with his fingers. All the while his revolver laden right hand stayed fixed, trained on her heaving chest.

Genevieve did as she was asked and walked over to the case, picking it up she turned on the spot. Fighting her fear she asked him some questions.

'What will happen to it?' she asked in trepidation. 'Where will it go? Who hired you? Was it the *Ordo Solis*?'

'You ask too many questions, senhorita.' he sneered in response. 'Where I take this is no concern of yours,' he raised his left hand ready to receive the case. 'As to who hired me. You seem to already know the answer to this, no?'

Genevieve bit her lip and frowned. 'You are an antiquities dealer, right?' she asked, 'If you give this to the church they will destroy it. This will be worth a small fortune.' She moved forward ever so slightly. 'If you let me take it, I can find more like it, I swear that we will give them to you.' She lied.

The large man laughed wistfully as he scratched his head with the barrel of his revolver.

'I am being compensated enough. And from what I have heard about you, you would never allow someone like me to take something as important as this.'

'How much are you getting paid?' she said, pulling the case back towards her chest.

Armon smiled indignantly and exhaled through his nose, 'More than you could pay.' He clicked his fingers impatiently and raised his chin gesturing to the case. 'No more games now senhorita. The Case.'

'And what if I were to put in a bid?' came a voice from the next room. Armon spun, his arm raised, the grip on the revolver tightening.

'O que você está fazendo aqui?' Spat Armon in anger.
'What am I doing here...' replied Massimo to Armon's
question. 'I am looking after my investment.'
'What are you talking about?' snapped Armon, lowering his
revolver as he gesticulated with both hands.
'How much do you want for the case?' came the simple reply.
'I am in no mood to haggle idiota!' Armon stepped forward,
snatching the case from Genevieve's hands aggressively. As
he made for the door.
'Two million Euro?' called Massimo nonchalantly, scratching
his chiselled cheek with his thumb.
Armon stopped on the spot and turned his head back to the
Italian. 'You would pay that much for this?' he paused,
shaking his head, 'I think not.'
'Three million then.' replied Massimo calmly.
Armon seemed caught between a rock and a hard place. The
Italians bid was double what he was originally to be paid, but
why did he want it so much that he would pay so much for it
without so much as a quibble. His suspicion grew too great.
'Why are you so interested all of a sudden?' he called back.
His sallow eyes flitting to the case held tightly in his grasp.

Massimo walked forward with a gentle smile. 'I have become
intrigued by all of this.' he walked over to stand beside
Genevieve as he spoke. 'This *principessa* has me all excited. She
is on to something, something that I myself have been piecing
together for a long time.'
Armon put the case down onto the ground and lowered his
revolver, 'You are serious Lupo?' he asked hesitantly. 'No
tricks, no *a traição*?'
'Three million Euros in your account within five minutes if
you hand over the case and leave this young lady to me.'

Armon smiled, 'Ah!' he spat. 'Now I see Lupo. What it is that is really persuading your actions.' he laughed heartily. 'You make a good offer for the case,' he stopped and stared once more at Genevieve. 'But for this young one, you will have to pay more, much more.' he looked her up and down menacingly. 'She is like the young girls sold out of the Netherlands,' he laughed haughtily. 'You know the Netherlands and the United Kingdom have the highest rate of human trafficking. Third is Romania.' He picked up the case once more and stepped closer to her, his eyes wild and malicious. 'I would get a good price for you. She will cost you another three million,' he sneered pervertedly.

Massimo looked across to Genevieve, 'My mother taught me many things, Armon.' he said with a calm smile. 'And one that has always stuck with me is this…' He turned to face Genevieve, his hand raised to brush her disobedient hair back behind her ear. 'No lady is ever for sale.'
Within a second it was all over, Genevieve took in a deep breath and fell backwards onto the table out of shock, her hand knocking over the heavy brass desk lamp. She tried to scream but nothing came out of her dry mouth. Massimo had pulled out a silenced Sig Sauer P320 pistol and fired three successive shots into Armon's sweaty head. Each bullet hitting its mark with a "*thut, thut, thut*" as the Black Market Antiques dealer dropped to his knees, the Samsonite case and revolver hit the ground simultaneously before his large body slumped inelegantly to the side hitting the ground with a heavy thud.

He reholstered his pistol and turned back to Genevieve with a smile. 'Are you alright, amore?' he asked.
Genevieve just stared at him, this act of pure brutality was far from chivalrous. He had murdered this man right in front of her. She could already smell the coppery taint of blood from across the room where it pooled around Armon's lifeless body.

'So,' he smiled charmingly at her, 'I have been meaning to ask,-'

"Whack!" Genevieve kicked him square in the testicles sending him doubling over to the ground. She swung the fallen brass desk lamp with malice knocking Massimo down further.

She jumped up from the table and grabbed the case from Armon's feet making sure she didn't look at his upper half. She bolted for the door just as the wall beside her exploded in a cloud of dust. She spun to see Massimo standing upright, his silenced pistol raised to her head. 'Basta!' he spat, rubbing his nether regions as blood dripped from his scalp.

'Are you going to shoot me?' she asked him boldly.

He walked forward, his confident and cocky swagger all but gone. His eyes narrowed as he approached her. 'You are lucky I like you Principessa.' he snarled as he came closer. 'If I wanted you would already be dead! I have let you live for a reason.'

She scanned the room desperately looking for an idea, her mind racing. She bit her lip then she saw it. She hit the light switch on the wall beside her, sending the room into darkness as she lurched out through the door into the external corridor. She now lay face down, slipping as her feet scrambled to get a grip on the marble floor, she got to her knees as she heard Massimo's sprinting footsteps running across the darkened room, she heard him slip momentarily on the blood pool by Armon's dead body.

But a man like this would not be stopped so easily, she knew full well that he would be on her in seconds. She managed to get a grip and rolled onto her front as Massimo's angered face appeared through the darkness only feet away on the other side of the door frame. His pistol appeared by his side. His feral eyes pierced through the darkness, he cursed repeatedly under his breath as he tried to come through the lab door frame.

His body suddenly bent over as he clenched his stomach, desperately winded he looked up to see Cortez stood on the other side of the door, crowbar still in hand like a baseball player who had just swung his bat for a homerun. But instead of a baseball he had connected with the Italian's throbbing insides. The Italian hesitated but managed to grab the iron crowbar that had just been savagely thrust into his abdomen, stopping Cortez from taking a second swing. But he was unable to retrieve it from the larger man's vice-like grip.

The sudden unforeseen impact had left Massimo momentarily immobile, his bruised diaphragm struggling to take in a steady breath. He stood hunched with his head at the same height of the door handle, his leather soled blood soaked shoes slipping on the highly polished marble effect floor tiles as though it were ice.

The irate Italian looked up and paused to see Cortez's large tattooed hairy fist come hurtling at his nose with a devastating speed. Too fast to attempt a block, and too breathless to move all he could do was wince in anticipation.
"Smack!"

Massimo was spun back through the doorway as Cortez pulled the office door shut feeding the large crowbar through the d-shaped door handle so that the crowbar was now resting tightly against the door frame locking the Hitman inside the darkened office. Cortez picked up Genevieve under his arm and half carried her along the corridor, they didn't even chance a look back as they spirited away out of the lab office.

One minute later Massimo had managed to kick the door open, splintering its wooden frame, he peered out to find the corridor deserted.

He placed a hand either side of his busted nose and clicked it back into its correct location and screamed in primaeval anger at his predicament as blood still gushed from his smashed nose and lacerated scalp. He hurt all over, his head, chest, stomach and groin all throbbed, he felt nauseous and weak. But his rage pushed him on. He could not afford to stop, not even for a second. He knew the consequences should he fail again.

They had escaped... again. But not only that, he had killed the man he had assumed was his current employer, even in the murdering world this was still a significant faux pas. His reputation was what kept him in work, and what kept him alive. If people found out he had killed Armon Da Silva he wouldn't be trusted to work again.

*

Cortez started the engine and slammed the Tesla into action, the enhanced battery power making them feel like astronauts during lift off. Zero to sixty in mere seconds. The silent wheels kicked up the dust and old discarded newspaper pages from the pavement as it whizzed through the busy student car park. Genevieve felt sick, the adrenaline making her racing mind nauseous.

'He just killed Armon.' she spoke after some time. 'He just shot him then tried it on with me like he was some kind of fucking hero.'

Cortez looked across at her, she was a real mess, but he knew how to handle her when she was like this. She had been through so much already today that this was the proverbial final straw that was about to break the camel's back. First Westminster, then Stirling's manor and now she had just watched a man lose half his face before being chased by a psychopath.

He drove into a small alleyway and parked up, killing the lights they were in total darkness. They had gone almost five miles from the university now and there was no sign of anyone following them. He unbuckled his seat belt, lifting up the central armrest that covered the void where the gear stick and hand brake usually lived in normal cars and slid over to her. He wrapped his large arms around her and pulled her in tight. He could feel the damp trickle of her tears on his neck as she nestled close to him and began to sob deeply.

'You are safe now Genny, I've got you.' he said in an almost whisper. He held her for several minutes letting her get it all out of her system. When she was ready he would stop, but he would let her lead. Their relationship over the past five years had seen them thrown into lots of similar predicaments where they had been shot at, chased or kidnapped by nefarious organisations, but it all still has an effect on you. His experience in the military on operations and special forces selection training gave him an edge, a hard shell exterior and upper hand and he knew exactly how to handle and harness the adrenaline, fear and excitement that races through your body and turns your stomach and your legs to jelly. But he understood that his companion was not trained or experienced and this was not easy for her. He gave her all the time she needed and when she was ready she lifted her head up and looked into his furry face and smiled weakly.

'Thank you' she said softly as he handed her a tissue to wipe her reddened eyes and streaming nose.
'I will always be here for you Genevieve.' he said calmly in reply, her eyes making a double take as she heard him say her full name, this was a seldom occurrence. He gently brushed her hair away from her eyes revealing her beautiful face as he smiled back at her.

She leant in closer biting her lip, her eyes were focused and infatuated as she moved in to kiss him softly on the mouth. He instantly closed his eyes and kissed her back, she could feel his large chest swell as he put his arms around her waist and upper back holding her in a protective embrace.

Their drive back to London was without incident, Cortez had received word that Flint was happy to meet them. It had been nearly eight months since their last encounter. Genevieve and Cortez had been searching for the 13th century Canonbie Jet Rosary beads that were stolen from the National Museum of Scotland in Edinburgh. Their hunt led them to Cambridge where an old associate of Genevieve's had heard rumours that they were about to be sold in a secret auction. This was where they first met Flint. An extremely cautious, conspiracist and secretive man, he lived and dressed like a film noir spy, dark trilby, beige trench coat and horn-rimmed sunglasses. Always off grid, no internet footprint and impossible to get hold of.

Flint had been the one who had mentioned the hidden words beneath words on manuscripts to Genevieve. He showed her an example from a 14th century text and she then followed her own clues that led her to the archive room at the British Museum that started the entire endeavour and search for the Goddess Path.
Cortez had hoped their meeting would be beneficial and that Flint would answer some of their many questions.

*

University of Essex Colchester Campus Car Park

'Fanculo!' shouted Massimo as he dropped Armon's heavy dead body into the boot of the late Antiquities Dealer's car. He rolled his shoulders back in protest from lifting the weight of the dead man. 'Grosso pezzo di merde!' he cursed as he slammed the door down.

He moved to the back seat where he pulled out a large holdall, unzipping it he found a change of clothes. He promptly removed his blood soaked shirt and jacket and slipped on the large black turtleneck sweater. This was definitely not his style of clothing, but it would be much less inconspicuous until he could get back to London and one of his caches. A man in his position always had items squirrelled away, clothes, phones, money, passports, and of course weaponry.

He knew that his targets would be heading back to London, thanks to a tip off from his handler. All he had to do was find them again.
The pain that ran through his entire throbbing, aching body was no short of agony. His gut stung and cramped from Cortez's crowbar, his nose was burning and his eyes watering, not from tears, this was just what happens when you have a trauma to the nose. His head screamed from the brass lamp and he didn't even want to think about his groin.
Massimo honestly felt sorry for himself for the first time in many years.

Something had changed inside his very core that had made him not complete his task. He closed his eyes in anguish as he contemplated what was going on. Why had he not just shot his targets back at Westminster.
Massimo rubbed his eyes and face and sat in the driver's seat. Checking his mobile phone he could see several missed calls. Through gritted teeth he dialled the number back.

'Pronto?' Came the low digitally distorted voice through the phone.

'È Massimo.' he replied hesitantly.

'È fatto? Is it done?' questioned the low voice.

He looked back to the boot of Armon's car, 'There has been a complication…'

He was met with silence, the awkwardness making him shift in his seat.

'What sort of complication?' asked the low voice.

'They killed Armon Di Silva.' he said with a raised eyebrow, hoping his lie would stick.

More silence, then a cold reply, 'Mere collateral damage.'

Massimo sighed silently with relief on hearing these words.

'Did you acquire the item in Armon's absence?' asked the low voice.

'Yes.' he lied. 'I have it with me. Do you want me to destroy it?'

'No, we would appreciate it if you could return it to Roma.' the voice seemed relieved. 'This has changed things, Lupo. Changed for the better, well done.'

Massimo remained silent.

'And the targets?' asked the low voice.

'I am in the process of taking care of them now, they are within my grasp and firmly in my sights. I will call as soon as they have been eliminated.' he replied enthusiastically.

'Very well, the clock is ticking Signor Lupo.' Then the line cleared.

Massimo knew that his time was running out. He knew there would be more *Ordo Solis* agents after him as soon as they realised he didn't have the case or eyes on either of his targets.

For now he had another job to do, one that he had been planning for weeks. He knew deep down that it was most likely linked to all the other targets he had eliminated over the past few months. But he still couldn't figure out how, or why for that matter.

'London's calling.' he said as he started Armon's car.

*

Chapter 8
In Like Flint

Dave's Diner, Nondescript Cafe, London

Genevieve and Cortez entered the address they had been
given, a dank and greasy looking diner tucked in a back street
away from prying eyes. The interior was dated, grubby and in
need of a good clean. It sported a dozen tables arranged
around the rectangular room, cheap chairs sat either side of
each table. Half empty crusted bottles of ketchup, brown
sauce and salt and vinegar adorned each table.

They sat in the centre at a small wobbly table and looked
around to see a chubby, balding man in a striped apron
standing behind the deli counter watching the football on a
television bolted to the wall. Otherwise they were alone in the
café. They ordered two coffees to the annoyance of the balding
man who didn't take his eyes off the football. The toilet door
suddenly opened as a slim man walked out. He was white, in
his mid sixties and appeared shifty as hell. He had the
appearance of the person that would be reported to the police
for lingering outside of schools. He wore a black under
armour baseball cap, sunglasses and long beige trench coat,
his hands firmly in his coat pockets.

'Flint…' said Cortez, nodding to the mysterious man standing
watching them. 'Good to see you again.'

Flint stood with his back to the wall, his hands deep in his
pockets, his feet wide apart. He appeared to be grinding his
teeth together as his narrow blue eyes scanned the unoccupied
room. 'I am glad you accepted my proposal.'

He was well spoken and eloquent, but spoke very fast. A tell-tale of someone on the Autistic spectrum or a habitual user of Class-A drugs, in Flint's case it was an unhealthy mixture of both.

Once he was content that nobody had followed the two of them inside the café he approached their table and sat facing the door. He shifted his glance around the room several times before starting, 'Let's be clear, if I sense something is awry I am gone.' He removed his sunglasses, his piercing blue eyes flitted between them as he spoke.

Genevieve furrowed her eyebrows and spoke softly, 'Thank you for agreeing to see us Mr Flint. I hope that you have been keeping well.' she started cautiously. 'Do you remember back in Cambridge, the symbolism that concealed the hidden text?' she pulled out a piece of paper as she spoke. 'It was inspirational,' she allowed a smile. 'I had a hunch about an old Lindisfarne text that seems to coincide with your alternate history of Britain. We wanted to talk to you about your theory on the Goddess Path and what you know about the Roman temple beneath St Pauls.' She held up the scribbling of her Latin translation, 'I found these words hidden beneath an open eye symbol, just like the one you showed me,' She handed him the piece of paper as his glass-like eyes scanned over it.

His unambiguous voice read the words, 'Between Minsters East and West lies the King's secret confessors know best.' His yellowing teeth appeared through a simpered smile.

The balding man brought their coffees over, as Cortez noticed the multiple suspect stains on his apron. He nodded his thanks but pushed the cup away in fear of what he might catch from drinking it.

'You have heard about my papers on the hidden Goddess Path?' Flint smiled broadly as he exhaled in delight. 'Oh, yes…You seek the truth.' He began nodding to himself. He took out a small console from his pocket and tapped the screen holding it up in front of both of them in turn. Satisfied with whatever it was doing, he then continued, 'Alright, Minsters east and west… So you want to know the truth of St Pauls and St Peters, that they are built on ancient temples that formed a section of the ancient stone pathway used by millions of women for well over twenty thousand years. What you don't know is that the history of these temples and the purpose of the stone pathway or Goddess Path as our ancestors called it, has been hidden from common knowledge. All tales and oral traditions silenced, all ancient texts and documentation re-written by those that are united beneath the Crossed Keys, the ancient Order of the Sun or *ordo solis* as they are known.'

'The Catholic Church?' affirmed Cortez.

'Exactly.' nodded Flint. 'History has been sculpted and manipulated by those in power to enforce and control their ideology.' He paused, taking a slurp of his grey tea. 'Their usual method is to make themselves out as the aggrieved victim, ensuring the steadfast support and resolute blessings of their devoted acolytes, sympathisers and idiotic followers.'

Genevieve was taken aback by the man's comment, 'Idiotic is rather a harsh term Mr Flint.' She challenged him. 'Religion teaches people moral behaviour, it builds society.'

Flint stared at her, his icy cold eyes blinking rapidly. 'Harsh?' he retorted, abashed by her comment. 'What would you call those that purposefully ignore science and advancements in technology and medicine? Hmm? Those that reject evolution, dinosaurs, history and archaeological evidence. Those that willingly encourage the unbalance and intolerance of other faiths? Hmm? Those that brutally enforce their lies with fear, control, hatred, separatism, manipulation and abuse?' Flint shouted back. His eyes flitted left and right. 'More lives have been lost in the so-called *name of religion* than any other cause Miss Silankis.'

Cortez and Genevieve exchanged a quick glance, thinking it best to just continue their questioning. This man's changeable characteristics and erratic behaviour was so unpredictable that his volatile and capricious mood could erupt at any minute.

'Tell us about the Roman temple at St. Pauls?' asked Genevieve. She took a sip from her coffee and instantly spat it back into the cup, she closed her eyes pulling a gagging face. She quickly pushed the cup away as Flint started to speak.

'What was found beneath St. Pauls was simply epic. An impressive ancient temple built by the Romans that stood on an even more impressive earlier Pagan site. The ancient site was incorporated into the new religion, encouraged by the Romans who worshipped the original feminine holy trinity. The Capitoline Triad.'

Flint raised one finger on his left hand, 'One,' he counted, 'The goddess Minerva, the Roman goddess of girls and women, wisdom, justice, law, victory, and the sponsor of arts, trade, and strategy. Two,' he raised a second finger, 'Juno the goddess connected with all aspects of the life of women and marriage and Three, the god Jupiter or Jove, god of the sky, heavens and stars.' he finished with his third finger raised. 'Back then the female gods were equal to the male gods, if not more important! This was the same for the Greeks and Pagans. It was all about balance, equilibrium, harmony and respect. But that all changed in the 4th century...' he paused, a sincere yet bewildered look filled his face.

'Four hundred years before, 40,000 Romans arrived on English shores in AD 43, they moved swiftly across the country and by AD 44 they set about installing shrines and temples in prominent areas and along well tread routes. Their first official city or Roman colonia was Colchester, founded shortly after they landed.' He slurped more tea and wiped his mouth with the back of his hand. 'Do you have any idea as to why they chose Colchester as their first colony?' he asked but gave no time for them to answer. 'They were intrigued by what they discovered, Colchester was home to the sacrificial plinth. The end of the line if you will.' he wiped his nose and continued.

'Sacrificial plinth?' asked Genevieve, leaning forward.

'If you want to make an impression, you go big or you go home.' smiled Flint. 'And the Romans had no desire to leave this island abundant with resources.

They had heard about this odd little place across the sea from Gaul that had lush green forests, fields filled with livestock and earth bountiful in gold, silver, lead, iron, tin and salt.' he paused only to slurp his tea.

'Like most of the foreign lands, Britannia was a country filled with wonder, mythology and barbarity. The land was filled with ancient relics, alien landscapes, and mysterious stone structures. At Colchester the invading forces discovered thousands of deviant burials surrounding a series of standing stones. In the centre was a huge slab known to the locals as the Sacrificial plinth. The burials belonged to both animal and human.' he paused to let this sink in.

'They wanted to ensure the local tribe, the Trinovantes, knew who was in charge. So they raised the site to the ground and built a huge monument to Camulos, the God of War right where the plinth had stood for millenia. This was the focal point of the Camulodunum Forum positioned in the centre of the Roman settlement.'

Cortez raised his finger, 'That now sits underneath Colchester Castle.'

'They all do.' smiled Flint in reply. 'You name a castle, cathedral, church or manor house and I will bet my left ear that it sits atop an ancient Pagan site. The majority of which will align with the Goddess Path. A series of ancient standing stones that ran across the country from north to south, east to west. With multiple large stone circles staged along the routes.

The most famous of which is Stonehenge, largely due to it being one of the only survivors of the purge but back then there were hundreds of them, some even larger than Stonehenge.'

'Purge?' asked Genevieve. Her perceptive vast knowledge of history was being tested today. She doubted everything she heard, but all the signs seemed to make it all fit together somehow in striking realisation.

Flint sucked his teeth and continued, 'It was what the Church called it in the 4th Century, when they raised nearly all Pagan monuments, temples and sites from existence. When they hunted down and murdered all the Pagan priests and priestesses and made worshipping Paganism and any other religion that wasn't Catholicism or Christianity illegal. This was not just restricted to England, this happened all over the European continent.'

'Constantine the Great,' nodded Genevieve excitedly as a period of history she knew finally came up. She had studied history for years gathering insightful knowledge, and not knowing about something drove her crazy. 'His actions in Jerusalem had a devastating tidal wave effect across the Empire. He set about destroying all Pagan sites to construct temples for their new church and neo god.'

'You're an intelligent girl.' remarked Flint, 'What else did he impose? You know all about the hostility and segregation. Imposing biassed laws to ban all magic, curses and sacrificial rituals. His blatant support for uprising, posse raising and encouragement of mob attacks on non-Christians.'

'He sounds familiar… Fake news' smiled Cortez to himself, screwing up his hairy face.

Flint didn't even look at him. 'Where St. Pauls, well the original St. Pauls was built, stood one of said ancient sites that was dedicated solely to the female, for all women and girls first in adolescence, then young adulthood. It incorporated their transitions, through adolescence and puberty, their menstrual cycle, then the miraculous act of pregnancy and birth. It was a rite of passage, a route walked by all females at differing stages of their lives.

Emperor Claudius, or to use his full name Tiberius Claudius Caesar Augustus Germanicus, spent a total of 16 days in England. His love for history and fascination with the bizarre practices of the barbarian tribes of Britannia led him to riding the full extent of the stone pathways. On his sixth day touring his newly conquered land he came to a settlement on the great river where London or Londinium as it was soon to be known would be settled the next year in AD 47. It was here when he heard what the purpose of the procession was and the importance of the stones that he ordered the construction of the Temple of The Capitoline Triad. The three Roman Gods dedicated to all things feminine, he wanted to incorporate the power and influence of these stones and the temple that originally stood there. Claudius was a keen historian and author of dozens of volumes covering the history of Carthage, the Etruscans, the Roman Republic and even the Roman alphabet. Tacitus, the infamous historian, even used these volumes to support his own work. It is odd then that all written volumes on his successful Conquest of Brittania were *lost*.' said Flint with a sniff. Emphasising his last word *lost* with inverted commas hand gesture.

'The lost scrolls…' replied Genevieve, nodding along. 'After Nero took the throne from Claudius' following his mysterious death in AD 54, the majority of his history scrolls disappeared.'

Cortez put out his bottom lip and raised his eyebrows, 'You know, some say the scrolls perished in the eruption of Pompei in AD 79 where old Clavdivs was staying. They say he faked his own death by eating a supposed poisonous mushroom and secretly moved to a private villa in Pompei and lived the life of a scholarly hermit with only his scrolls, wine and his trusted slave and lover.' Cortez smiled proudly only to become awkwardly silent as both Genevieve and Flint just stared at him in silence. 'It's just a conspiracy, thought you might have been interested.' His face reddened as he went to take a swig of his coffee before he managed to stop himself. He called over to the dirty apron guy, 'You got anything in a can, you know sealed?'

Flint once again ignored him and continued to speak, 'On his return to Rome Claudius was awarded the triumphal arch on the Via Flaminia in AD 51. The relief displayed the new feminine temple and standing stones standing side by side. These have all but fallen into ruin following the many sackings but I have seen engravings from the eighth century when Charlemagne conquered Italy and Rome in AD 778. He renovated much of the ruined city and sent out architects and scholars to record what they could. The arch was later chiselled away and reset with plain mortared walls sometime over the next twenty-two years prior to when Charlemagne was crowned the Holy Roman Emperor in St. Peter's Basilica.'

'You have seen an engraving of the temple?' asked Genevieve, gobsmacked.

'Indeed, Miss Silankis… I have. I have also seen Wren's original reports on the Goddess Path temple. After the great fire of 1666, all the charred building remains were levelled revealing the ruins of the Roman temple beneath. The church was called upon to see what was uncovered. True to their nature of self preservation they destroyed the Roman remains and the remaining standing stones that were housed in the entrance of the Roman temple. But not before Wren had drawn several sketches and written his reports to Sir Isaac Newton, his trusted friend and contact at The Royal Society of London for Improving Natural Knowledge. In June 1675 Wren started the building we know today, but this time after some deliberation he moved it further south to avoid the poor marshy ground quality and copious risks of flooding.'

'Where was Wren's report?' asked Cortez.

'You mean, where is Wren's report?' answered Flint wryly.

'It still exists?' gasped Genevieve, now excited. 'Where is it?'

'It lies in the vaults of The Royal Society at Carlton House Terrace, London.' he replied. 'The Order of the Sun has been harassing the Society for centuries trying to gain access to their records and archives, they even tried to burn it to the ground before, back when Newton started all his Gravity theories. But thankfully to no avail.' Flint looked at them both, at their wide eyes of intrigue and shook his head, 'And no, before you ask. I would not be able to get you in to look at it…' He coughed awkwardly, 'I have been banned for life… But we will not be discussing that here.'

'There have been countless attempts at releasing this information to the world, but all those that try either disappear or end up dead. There are those that have tried to rise up against The Order of the Sun, some you would have heard of, Edward The Confessor, Anglo-Saxon King Harold Godwinson, Sir Francis Drake, Alison Askew, Guy Fawkes, Lady Diana Spencer.' he stopped and shook his head solemnly. 'And there are thousands that you wouldn't have heard of. Those that kicked the hornets' nest and got well and truly stung.'

'Guy Fawkes?' they retorted aghast. 'He was a Catholic apologist and martyr.'

'Oh yes, that was a real shit show.' started Flint, slurping more of his grey tea. 'Long story short, Guy Fawkes wasn't looking to blow up Parliament for the Catholic Church, he was STRONGLY against the totalitarian church and Parliament's misogynistic views and oppressive treatment of women. It had nothing to do with the persecution of Roman Catholics by the English government and crown. This was simply just another fabrication to make the church the victim. Fawkes's true agenda was down to the liberation of the female population from the oppression and sexual discrimination from the men ruling the country. It is right to say that the thirteen men directly involved in the Gunpowder Plot were all linked to influential and aristocratic Catholic families. But who wasn't back then? Powerful families rose and fell every few years as the religious upheaval devastated the country. The power flitted back and forth so much during The Protestant Reformation that you simply had to say you were linked to Catholic and Protestant families depending on which monarch was in power. It just depended on where you were stood and who you were saying it to.'

'After James, King of Scotland reassured Thomas Percy that he would relax the restrictions and laws persecuting the female Catholics and offer them safety and equality when he came into power. Percy shared the new found promises with his family and friends, only for King James to deny any such promise of impartiality when he took the throne in 1603. Much like Constantine the Great thirteen hundred years before, stricter laws against women were enforced and Percy sought revenge and rallied to enlist his fellow supporters at the Duck and Drake Inn in London in May 1604. Percy leased a house near to Parliament buildings where works started on a tunnel to the House of Lords. Beneath which, they knew lay the original temple of the Goddess Path. They wanted to unearth the temple and make its importance known to all. To resuscitate what had been smothered for so long, to release the harmony of equality within all religion.'

'What the Order of the Sun hadn't figured out was that for months a plot was schemed to take out select figures that would in part put into action the revolution and installation of equal rights amongst both the sexes and multi faiths throughout the populaces. If they had heard about the plot to unearth the long-hidden Goddess Path and its significance the church would have the schism of the millenia on their hands. Can you only imagine an all female led Europe.' he laughed to himself. 'Perfection.' He flashed his yellowing teeth as he looked Genevieve up and down.

'How so?' interjected Cortez, he leant in closer ensuring Flint was now looking at him.

'Percy's intention was to remove James and his Parliamentary followers and install Princess Elizabeth, James's nine-year-old daughter as Queen of England and Scotland.

The plan was to secure a female led nation by marrying her off to the son of Spanish King Philip III who had in part been fed lies to suggest he fund and supply soldiers to help instil a Catholic monarch by removing James from the throne. The next step would be to remove Philip and his sons leaving Ana María Mauricia, the King's four year old daughter to rule Spain. Guy Fawkes spent many years living and serving for the Spanish army and became an expert in explosives and gunpowder. He adopted the name "Guido" to fit in with his fellow conscripts. He took a Spanish lover who introduced him to a powerful group of what we would today call intellectual feminists that held great power, prominence and sway within Spanish politics and the crown. He came back to England with this knowledge and suggested to Percy that they unite the English, Scottish and Spanish under this very ideology, revealing the Goddess Path back to the populace. New rule, new religion, new world.'

'So Fawkes wasn't going to use the gunpowder at Westminster?' asked Cortez, now confused.

Flint licked his lips and looked mischievous whilst he spoke, 'The original plan was for Percy's men, accompanied by two dozen other soldiers, to storm Parliament and run them all through.' his eyes lit up as he said this. 'But when John Whitgift died in February 1604, they had to change tack so Robert Catesby came up with plan B, bring on the gunpowder.

Through the eavesdropping of his female contacts acting as domestic house staff for several members of Parliament that he had clandestinely installed and hidden in plain sight within the very houses and manors of his intended targets a great revelation came to his ears.'

'Both King James I and the head of the Catholic Church in England would be at the same location at the same time. Within the very walls of Parliament. Catesby and Fawkes wanted to take out both Richard Bancroft who was the newly appointed Archbishop of Canterbury who was the "Primate of All England", and James I the King of England and Scotland, notably a man who shared the misogynistic views of the Church. If their plan were to succeed they would also take out all opposing hostility from parliament, unveil the ancient Goddess Path temple beneath and be in possession of Claudius' scrolls, legitimate documentation that credited the temple's authenticity. Three bird's one big explosive stone.' Flint slurped his drink, wiping his mouth with the back of his hand. 'It's marvellous isn't it?' he grinned excitedly.

'Bit of a gamble blowing it all up…' started Cortez, raising an eyebrow. 'Could accidentally destroy the temple in the process.'

'That was why they were digging the tunnel to locate the Claudius scrolls and the precise location of the Goddess Path temple. So they knew exactly where to place the explosives so as not to damage the ancient structure, but at the same time, take out the king, archbishop and antagonistic MPs.' beamed Flint,

'All was going to plan until March 1605 when the tunnel they were digging to access the lost Goddess Path temple was abandoned after running into difficulties, instead they decided to rent a coal storeroom below the King's throne room at the House of Parliament.

It was close enough to the chambers where their targets would be located, and high enough not to cause damage to the foundations or the underlying temple. By July 1605 Thirty-six barrels of powder were stored and sat ready to remove their targets and change the world as they knew it.'

Genevieve held up her palm, she tried with all her exhausted might to calm her racing mind. 'Hang on…' she paused, 'So, you are telling me that if all of this had gone to plan, there would have been an orchestrated total restructuring of monarchies across Europe, the re-introduction of an ancient female led religion and the unveiling of Mesolithic temples across England.' She looked at Flint agog. 'And their insurance was to use a sixteen hundred year old scroll written by Emperor Claudius?' She could hardly believe what she was hearing.

'Told you it was a good story, didn't I?' laughed Flint, his wheezy aqualung cough reflecting how much he smoked. 'It would have all worked out if it hadn't been for one man, Francis Thresham, the git.' spat Flint. 'Thresham notified his brother-in-law Lord Monteagle two weeks before the scheduled opening of parliament on the 5th November 1605. Tresham hand delivered the note to Monteagle's home in Hoxton, North London, on 26th October 1605. The letter was received by Monteagle's prying servant, a self righteous and sanctimonious man named Ward.

Ward's probing nature meant that he kept an eye on his master's private affairs, resulting in him opening and reading the letter. Ward was in the pocket and regular recipient of an informant's purse from Robert Cecil, Earl of Salisbury, the King's most important minister.

Ward immediately contacted Cecil who informed the authorities and ultimately King James. The trap was set and the rest is history. Guido was captured searching for the Claudius scrolls on the Goddess Path and the Temple that sat beneath the Minsters. As he had already been barred from Parliament for his questionable loyalties to Spain he gave the false name John Johnson to the arresting guard. He was quickly identified and tortured by the Order for two whole days. They broke that man in unimaginable ways, using barbaric and inhumane interrogation methods. But still, he remained quiet and refused to divulge the location of the Claudius scrolls. They still remain hidden almost four hundred years later.

'How do you know all of this?' asked Genevieve.

'My grandmother was Suffragette Marjory Hume. She knew the location and attempted to remove the scrolls on 27th April 1909 but was challenged by the attending MP's and the Parliamentary security. To ensure they didn't glean what she was doing there she chained herself to the statue as an act of protest for her Suffragette cause.' Flint placed an old photograph down onto the table beside his drink and smiled.

'Oh my goodness, I know this statue...' spluttered Genevieve standing up, she paced the empty café taking out her phone holding it to her ear. 'I need to call someone.' as she turned away from them as she began to speak into her handset.

'Oh and Cortez,' snapped Flint in a hushed voice, taking him by the arm, whispering softly into his ear, 'You are correct in your theory on Claudius, he lived in peace for twenty-five years at his secret villa. Only to succumb to the fatal force of Vesuvius.' he winked knowingly.

*

Nondescript Road, London

Massimo watched the busy street below; throngs of people aimlessly coming and going, absorbed and oblivious in their phones, their shopping, walking their dogs, and socialising. He scanned their faces from his vantage point until he saw who he was looking for. He released a smile and raised his silenced assault rifle up to his shoulder, levelled the Advanced Combat Optical Gunsight (ACOG) scope to his eyeline and found the jogging target, now centred perfectly through his crosshairs. From this short distance he didn't need to worry about forward allowance, the distance around the target that you would allow if they were in movement.

You shoot where the target is going and not where it is now. But this target was jogging slowly, he judged an approximate steady 8 kph. He adjusted the scope's magnification as the view of his target changed with a flick instantly enlarging from the sweat soaked torso to a close up of his target's face.

Revealing an incredibly high definition magnification of a sweat covered ruddy face, open mouthed puffing and panting, a droplet of snot dangled precariously from their columella. 'Crack'.

The shot was not even audible outside due to the heavy traffic rumbling past, no one noticed anything for several seconds. Then the screams began, and the panic ensued as chaos erupted. Massimo bent down to collect the shell casing from the floorboards, dismantled the rifle and put on his suit jacket, all within ten seconds. Shouldering his holdall he walked casually down, out and away from the building via the opposite side, disappearing into the crowds traipsing the pavements.

'It is done.' he said coldly, his hands free earpiece flashing blue as he spoke.

'Bravo Massimo.' replied the elderly voice. 'And our other problem?'

'I am heading to St. Stephen's Chapel now.' he replied, checking his watch, 'In twenty minutes all will be done.'

'Andare con Dio.' replied the elderly voice before it disconnected.

Massimo watched as an ambulance raced past him, blue lights and sirens blaring. Heading to where he had just left. Minutes later two Metropolitan police cars raced past.

He raised an eyebrow at the speed in which the emergency services had arrived at the scene. He had not expected them this quickly but he was already a quarter mile away. He took out his mobile and opened the folder containing his target's details. His thumb paused over the smiling photograph before he clicked the delete button.

Another face to haunt his subconscious, another face to find him in his dreams. His phone buzzed as he glimpsed the message pop up confirming payment. €250,000 for what appeared to be a simple five minute job, "what a way to make a living." some said. But he had always resented people's misconstrued and uneducated opinion of being an assassin. They never take into account the hours watching, planning and learning.

This target for instance, he had to follow for two weeks to know the best spot to identify the routine, the repetitive nature, the characteristics that he could manipulate and use to his advantage. The planning for the location, finding a discreet spot to carry out the hit. If people only knew how hard it is to find somewhere that is not covered in CCTV in a city that has more cameras than the Chinese Secret Service. To find a vantage point that was unoccupied or monitored, an entrance that was not seen by potential witnesses or idiots recording on their social media accounts as they walked past him.

This target was under surveillance 24/7, personal bodyguards went everywhere with them, their home was guarded, their office practically impenetrable. The only time he could get close or take the shot was during the tri-weekly run that happened at the same time every Monday, Wednesday and Saturday.

Massimo had quickly seen that the target's escort always fell behind along this road. They had become complacent, lazy and reliant on the fact that nothing had happened during these frequent runs.

The sheer volume of pedestrians and food and market stalls outside of the foreign stores held them up, and they made no effort to catch up with their employer. The armed escort was just over four metres away behind the surging crowds and Massimo knew their visibility on their charge would have been nil, they would have only discovered their charge was in trouble or dead from the screams that quickly echoed from ahead of them. By the time they had pushed through and reached them, there would be no life saving opportunities and Massimo would have already evacuated the building on the other side of the adjacent road.

He opened the next file on his phone to reveal a photograph of a young woman, mid thirties, fiery red hair, suited, she had educated sharp green eyes, standing in front of the infamous statue lined corridor of stained glass windows of St. Stephen's Hall in Westminster.

The walk kept him alert, as more police vehicles passed him he knew he could not mess this next stage up. Failure now would cost him his life. He could not fail. He would normally disappear within the crowds, blend in and become almost invisible. But today he stood out, his nose and eyes heavily bruised, he looked awful. And every person he passed in the street made an effort to side step him making his chameleon training almost impossible.

He walked across Great Smith Street and stopped at the sight of blue flashing lights surrounding Westminster. 'Cazzo!' he spat as he slowed his pace. Peering around the corner he took in the situation. *Hostile Reconnaissance* he called it. It was what kept him alive.

Across the street he saw the three armed units now standing guard at the entrance of The Westminster Abbey Shop, pointing to the arch to their right that led into Dean's Yard and the main entrance into Westminster behind the gate to their left. The three units then split up jogging to their respective entrances.

Massimo paused in thought for a moment. Then looked up, he allowed a small smile before re shouldering his holdall so that it would not move during his ascent. He jumped up to grip the decorative stone architrave that followed the shape of the brown wooden emergency exit door below.

He nimbly climbed up to the first window directly above that had been left ajar. He glimpsed the stone relief just above him that read, "*Q.A.B Rebuilt 1900*". He had gone from pavement to inside in seven seconds without a single person seeing him.

He closed the front door to number 3 on the opposite side of the building, taking care to hide his face from the CCTV camera to his right. He walked calmly across Dean's Yard, the soft turf felt springy beneath his designer shoes. He headed for the Cellarium Cafe & Terrace directly across and slipped into the rear of the café via a fire door that had been propped open by one of the hapless staff.

The presence of the emergency services and armed response had cleared the entire area of all tourists. Tables covered in delectable foods and drinks, but the chairs sat empty. He burst into spontaneous song with a line from one of his favourite musicals,

'Phantom faces at the window, Phantom shadows on the floor,
Empty chairs at empty tables, Where my friends will meet no
more.'

The beautiful, vaulted ceilings and ancient doorways framed
the contemporary café, he glanced around and shrugged his
shoulders, it looked like a nice enough place. He paused at
one of the now vacant tables to see a small Espresso coffee,
neglected and forgotten by the previous customer. Testing it
was still hot with his fingertip he sipped it, but regretted it
instantly. 'Che schifo…' he spat it back into the small cup.
'No'. Placing it back on the table he rolled his eyes. 'So hard to
find a decent coffee in this country.'

He continued his way through towards the desolate and
vacant Abbey cloisters that adjoined the restaurant.

The sun shone brightly through the stone arches of the
covered walkway that edged the central lush green quad. He
tutted to himself playfully as he passed the door that led back
through to Chapter House and Pyx Chamber, remembering
the last time he had entered there with Genevieve and Cortez.

Keeping to the shadows he surreptitiously moved closer to the
Abbey's South Transept. The place was completely deserted,
making his route to the easternmost part of the Abbey
through the brass gates to the Lady Chapel surprisingly easy.

Massimo paused, taking some time to appreciate the
spectacular hand-carved fan-vaulted tracery ceiling that
spread across the entire chapel.

He admired the stained glass window at the far east end. He took in the ninety-six original Tudor saints and prophet statues that stood watch below the tall windows. Then looked down the chapel to the tomb of Henry VII and his wife, Elizabeth of York. 'Che figata!' Built in 1503 the chapel was designed to establish the Tudor dynasty. Dedicated to the Virgin Mary it was the statement piece that secured the Tudor lineage, making it beyond contestation.

He walked the edge of the spacious chamber, letting his finger tips caress the hand crafted and age-worn unique Misericords above the hinged oak seats that ran either side of the Chapel's body. His father had told him about the Knights of Bath, how King George I had revived the ancient order in 1725 as a mark of the highest honour for his knights. He took in all the coat of arms flags that adorned the high ceiling above him, then he saw what he was after. He checked his phone for the image, held it up to take in the plethora of historic crested coat of arms painted onto one of the many oak panels above the seat plinths. 'Eccolo!' His hands found the Misericord that he was after, a partially damaged carving of a female monster holding something in her hand, beside a headless dragon.

The object in the abominable female figure's hand was an open book. Carefully he twisted the small oak carving of the book until it clunked to a stop. Pushing the small oak panel back several centimetres he engaged a hidden mechanism within the belly of the ancient oak panelling.

Behind him the central tomb of Henry VII released a sudden cracking sound making him spin on the spot. Like a startled cat his dark, bruised eyes scanned the empty chamber for signs of movement.

Forcing the black grilled gate open he made his way inside the monument proper. He glanced over Henry and Elizabeth's effigies laying atop the tomb. Stalking the monument he could see the black marble base was adorned with six large copper gilt medallions, one for each of Henry's patron saints. John the Baptist and John the Evangelist, Christopher, Mary Magdalene, Michael, Anthony, Vincent, George, Barbara and Edward the Confessor.

It was Edward the Confessors medallion that made him smile. The cracking sound had emitted from this very spot. The large copper gilded disc now sat slightly open. Pushing it fully back inside the monument he could see the entire tomb was empty. The bodies of both Elizabeth and Henry were in fact buried in a special vault many feet beneath their tomb, making them the first monarchs to be interred under the Abbey's floor, rather than inside the tomb.

His father had told him that during the Civil War, Oliver Cromwell and his puritans had destroyed the original altar and most of the tomb inside Lady Chapel. After the restoration of the monarchy in 1660, Charles II paid for the repairs and sought guidance from his intellectual friends. These friends were architects, mathematicians and scientists. Together they formed a guild and established the Royal Society, who in part advised Charles of the ancient secret underground tunnel that led beneath Abingdon Street and up into the Palace of Westminster.

Using the torch on his mobile phone he looked down to the staircase that led down into darkness below. Massimo climbed through the round opening and descended the hewn stone stairs two at a time, the cool damp air made the hairs on the back of his neck stand on end.

When his father had been teaching him about the historic Order of the Bath, he had also mentioned how through the years these tunnels had acted as safe passage for many. The most recent of which was Winston Churchill during the Second World War, this passage had been utilised to ensure messages reached the Prime Minister's private room inside the now infamous War Rooms beneath Westminster.

As Massimo descended he noticed how the aged damp masonry stones soon turned to the unmistakable grey finish of concrete. The walls transitioned into tiled walls that were littered with ducts, cables and pipework stretching off into the distance. The steel reinforced door signalled his arrival beneath Parliament in the Palace of Westminster. The rusted lock took seconds to open, but the seized hinges took more effort than he would have liked, not to mention the unwanted attention the squealing metal made as he pushed the door ajar.

He slipped on his Faraday gloves and moved silently through the neo-gothic building until he had reached his destination. The doors leading into St. Stephen's Hall. A single police officer stood guarding the doorway, his back to the Italian, his assault rifle harnessed over his shoulder and cuddled in front of his armoured hi-vis chest.

Massimo stalked forward like a panther, his posture squat, balanced and low, his stylish leather shoes prowling perfectly silent on the polished floor tiles. Now standing directly behind the nonchalant, oblivious police officer he rose to stand full height. A gloved hand now positioned either side of the officer's face. The only noise was from the shoulder strap of the assault rifle pulling taught as it now dangled freely. Dropped by the dead police officer.

Massimo slid the body off to the side of the corridor and through into a vacant room. Footsteps echoed from around the corner as he nestled in the darkness of the vacant room. He watched from the shadows, lying in wait until his target appeared.

The footsteps crescendoed as an attractive young lady appeared from the opposite end of the corridor. The young lady was on her mobile, walking at speed, her heeled shoes clomping the hard floor as she entered St. Stephen's Hall. 'Yes Genevieve, I am here. The statue is still intact.' she spoke hurriedly and in a state of panic.

On hearing Genevieve's name Massimo's eyes widened suddenly. He abandoned his hide and crept through the large wooden door behind her, taking cover behind the statue nearest the door. He wanted to hear everything that she was talking about.

'Yes, I will wait here for you, I have already spoken to Steve, our head of security on the main door, he will escort you inside.' She hung up and brushed her red hair from her face.

She huffed loudly and relaxed her suited shoulders. 'This is all I bloody needed today.' she cursed under her breath.

Massimo watched her in silence. He knew everything about her from the file he had received but he always liked to see his target for himself, use his own judgement. He made his move, several large strides and he was behind her, silenced pistol an inch from her frizzy hair.

She turned as he spoke, his voice almost a whisper. 'Hello Elizabeth.' Her eyes went wide and her mouth dropped as she leapt aside at the unexpected presence of a gunman behind her. She tried desperately to take several breaths in but her chest wouldn't cooperate. The sight of the gun had forced her into shock.

'How do you know my name?' she asked in agonal sharp gasps.

'Cappuccetto Rosso' he smiled sinisterly.

She looked at him with a puzzled look, 'Little Red Riding Hood?' she repeated in English.

'Very good,' he replied coolly, 'Well Miss Red Riding Hood, I am Mr Wolf.'

Elizabeth swallowed hard, her eyes fixated on the pistol now held in front of her eyes.

'Do you believe in coincidence Elizabeth?' His words were eerily harrowing, his eyes wide and bemused. 'Genevieve is a rare name, Elizabeth. This person you were just speaking to… Would this be Genevieve Silankis?' he asked, his face wincing slightly as he spoke, still bruised and darkened from Cortez's heavy blows. 'I said, do you believe in coincidence Elizabeth?'

He stepped closer to her making her squeal as she folded her arms tightly around her body in an act of futile self preservation.

Her eyes transfixed to the floor. Massimo had lost his usual charm and charisma, he was tired, in pain and needed results. He knew too well that his time was running out. 'I shall take your silence as a yes,' he continued, still whispering, 'The fact that you just said her name, has just saved your life.' He lowered his pistol and stepped back from her. He rubbed his stubbled chin and stared at Elizabeth then around the hall to the statues positioned either side.

'Now! Tell me Elizabeth, what is she coming here to see?' he asked more amicably this time. His contused face faking a smile.

Elizabeth stopped beside the Falkland Statue, 'This…' she stammered, 'This is Lucius Cary, the one I spoke about with Genevieve.' She placed her shaking hands upon the statue's base.

'What is its significance?' demanded Massimo. He looked the statue up and down for anything obscure or relevant to what he had previously learnt about the Neolithic path. He pushed at the five sided chest high stone plinth that housed the eight foot tall statue of a 16th Century gentleman holding a Cavalry sword, his right foot raised on a stone block.

'It was crafted by John Bell in 1845, it portrays Lucius Cary, 2nd Viscount Falkland 1610–1643, he died aged only 33 years old.'

'Who was he?' asked Massimo. He stared at the statue's face to try and read his features. He looked at the 17th century Mortuary cavalry sword resting beneath his hands, the raised right foot.

'He was a critical thinker, a rational avant-garde intellectual mind in an age dominated by chauvinistic intolerance and dogmatism.'

'Go on.' he encouraged, now intrigued.

'He was a Royalist who died fighting in the Civil War. He was a supporter of change and equality. You could call him an original Humanist.'

'So the really important question is, why is Genevieve so interested in this particular statue?'

*

Chapter 9
Yes, Minister

Dave's Diner, Nondescript Cafe, London

'Elizabeth has arranged access for us, she can take us directly to the statue.' smiled Genevieve as she returned to the table.

'Triffick.' replied Cortez sarcastically, scratching his beard. 'So all we need to do is fetch the Claudius Scrolls from inside this listed statue protected by armed police, then go to the Royal Society to steal a copy of Wren's original plans for the Goddess Temple from within the vaults at Carlton House, stop a psychopathic professional hitman from killing us and expose a super powerful, super-secret religious cult. All before releasing some mind blowing conspiracy about an ancient Mesolithic pathway onto the world.' he sighed defeatedly.

Flint nodded, 'Sounds like my sort of party.' he laughed maniacally. 'To get into the vault you will need to access a secure elevator to the basement level, then you will need biometric clearance from the Foreign Secretary of the Royal Society.' The two of them looked at him in astonishment. 'I have an inside man, so to speak.' he sniffed, tapping the side of his nose.
'The Foreign Secretary works as chief scientific advisor for the Ministry of Defence. His name is Major Calvin Montgomery. But he has gone off grid. He has bodyguards, home security and works in secret locations.'
'We know him.' snapped Genevieve, shooting a cautious look over to Cortez. 'We worked with him a few years ago.'
Cortez nodded with a wince as he rubbed his left shoulder. 'Call him.' he said, to Genevieve's shocked expression. 'Call him! He said again, reinforcing his nod assertively.

'I notice quite a bit of hesitation and hostility here.' remarked Flint openly.

Cortez nodded, chewing the side of his mouth, 'Yeah. Long story. The last time we spoke to Calvin he fractured my collarbone with a cricket bat…' Cortez looked across to a frustrated Genevieve.

'He isn't answering his phone, damnit!' shouted Genevieve angrily.

'We can go to his home, bang his door until he opens it.' encouraged Cortez removing the car keys as he spoke.

Genevieve's eyes shot to her left as she saw the news on the café television. The football had been interrupted by a breaking news report. The BBC anchor was wearing a black tie and resolute face of the utmost seriousness which never boded well. Then the screen shot to a cordoned off area and a large white CSI forensics tent. The austere face of Calvin Montgomery then appeared in the corner of the screen. Dressed in full military uniform.

'Oh my goodness, this is insane!' shouted Genevieve, suddenly feeling nauseous. She stood to walk towards the television, her mouth open.

'Can you turn that up mate?' asked Cortez, also making his way up to the counter, standing beside Genevieve.

The aproned man shrugged before flipping the remote as the news anchor's voice filled the empty café, *'The body has been identified as the disgraced United Nations army officer, Major Calvin Montgomery. Who was recently acquitted for multiple war crimes in Cyprus involving the July Massacre at the Turkish - Cypriot border. Witnesses state that the Major was enjoying his morning run when he was gunned down in a back street just off Battersea Park.'*

Genevieve turned white, she spun round to Cortez who had already rushed to her side, he held her close, tight in his arms.

He kissed her hair and gave her that gentle squeeze of reassurance. 'Sokay Genny, it's all going to be ok.' he whispered. His mouth pushed against her head.

Flint shook his head in disapproval, 'Those bastards.' he spat indignantly. 'Another one bites the dust.'

The news anchor continued to narrate the scene, then it cut to footage of Calvin Montgomery walking through crowds of protestors outside of The Hague, the words "Library Footage" displayed clearly across the bottom. '*At this time it is unknown who the suspect is, but mounting tensions between the Turkish and Cypriot nations following Major Montgomery's turbulent trial suggest that those responsible may belong to separatists from either side.*' The anchor continued to misconstrue their politically propaganda-fuelled misinformation about what they believed to have happened.

Genevieve puffed out her cheeks, rubbed her red eyes and wiped her nose on a napkin. 'We have to stop them.'
'We will stop them.' replied Cortez reassuringly.

'The only way to stop these people is to expose them. To succeed where hundreds have failed.' snarled Flint. 'You need to gather up as much evidence as you can and blow the lid on all of this.'

'How are we supposed to take on an organisation of this calibre?' snapped Genevieve cautiously. 'We are going to get ourselves killed.' she pointed to the television.

'Genny,' started Cortez, placing his hand on her forearm affectionately. 'We are in too deep to turn back now. Even if we ran away and went into hiding, these people will not stop until we are dead.'

'What about DI Thorgood?' asked Genevieve desperately. 'Surely she can help us with this?'

Cortez held her gaze but remained silent whilst he weighed up their options, all the possibilities and outcomes of their predicament. 'I will give her a call, see where we stand.'

Flint's wristwatch buzzed against the table, his erratic blue eyes glancing down momentarily before he stood up, put on his sunglasses and made his excuses to leave. 'I never stay in one place for more than one hour…' he glanced at the deserted café once more, his paranoia evident. 'It makes it harder for *them* to track you. Once you have all the evidence compiled, contact me. I will be able to help you expose them when you need it.' With this he walked out of the door, leaving them sitting at their table.

Genevieve sank her head into her hands, 'So he is just going to leave us?' she said emptily as the café door closed with a ding of the small bell.

Cortez took out his phone, hitting the dial button he placed the small device between his rounded muscular shoulder and his grizzly chin. 'It will be alright Genny.' he said as the phone connected.

'Sal, we need to talk. Shits just got real and we are really out of our depth here.' He was about to relay all the newly discovered information to his old friend but when she remained deathly silent on the receiver he hesitated. 'Sal, can you help?'

He waited for a response, but none came. 'Sal, you still there?' he asked sincerely. 'Sal?'

A new voice came through the mobile telephone, a voice he had never heard before. It was foreign, confident and authoritative.

Cortez pulled the phone away from his ear, switching it onto loudspeaker so Genevieve could hear it.

'Am I speaking to Mr Simon Lewes?' asked the unknown voice. 'Also known as Cortez?'

Cortez inhaled deeply, his appearance calm and collected but his mind was processing everything at a thousand miles per hour.

'Yeah, that's me,' he replied slowly. 'I can only assume that I am speaking to *Ordo Solis.*'

'Very good, that will save me time explaining.' replied the foreign voice. 'You know why we are calling?'

'I have a pretty good idea,' shot Cortez. 'Where is Sally Thorgood?' he asked inquisitively after his friend.

'She is unharmed, in fact, I have just been speaking to your associate Detective Inspector Thorgood here about your little adventure.' said the voice.

'Let me speak to her.' demanded Cortez.

'Cortez, I am fine.' came Throgood's voice through the handset.

'How's the weather there Sal?' asked Cortez, looking serious.

'Looks like rain to be honest.' she replied. 'And silly me, forgetting my umbrella.'

Cortez closed his eyes before he replied. 'Who am I speaking to?' asked Cortez strongly.

'My name is not important. What is important is who I represent Mr Lewes. I am speaking to you on behalf of an interested party, those that are after what you currently have in your possession.'

'And what might that be exactly?' asked Cortez coolly.

'Let's not play games here Mr Lewes,' snapped the unknown voice, the inflection changing to a tired tone. 'You have what we want. I am going to give you an ultimatum, you will then have ten minutes to decide how we progress with this situation. I will be frank with you as I know you are not a man on whom I should waste time. We have the means to take this item from you, whether you agree to it or not. But, I want to give you the opportunity to make the right decision.'

'This is all very intriguing mate, but it sounds to me that either way I lose.' retorted Cortez. 'What are your terms?'

'Option one, you bring the items to me and you and Miss Silankis walk away. Option two,' he continued, 'You continue this futile scenario in playing a game that you will ultimately lose.'

Cortez muted the phone so he could speak freely with Genevieve. She had remained silent throughout the conversation to ensure they didn't know she was present. 'I'm going to be honest with you Genny, Sal is in trouble. I have to go and help her. I got her into this and I can't have her getting caught up in my mess.'

'Didn't she just say that she was fine?' asked Genevieve openly, her face showing her confusion.

'Looks like rain.' he replied knowingly. 'Our little code. She is being held against her will and things look dire. No umbrella means she is unarmed.'

Genevieve just looked dispiritedly across at her old friend. His past was still a mystery to her, the things he had done, the things he knew.

Even after all these years she realised he was still a stranger, yet she felt so close to him. His entire manner was repressed and guarded, letting no one get too close to him.

'Where do we go from here?' she asked solemnly.

He unmuted the phone and held it in front of his mouth, 'You said we have ten minutes, so I am going to take them. Hold on.' he said before he re-muted it.

Looking Genevieve directly in the eye he asked her, 'I need to know that you consent 100% on this Genny.' he paused for a second, rubbing his thumb on her small soft hand on the sticky café table between them. 'If you have any hesitations you need to tell me now.'

She bit her lip, contemplating their choices. She nodded and let out a reassuring smile.

'Whatever we do, I want to do it with you... together.' she replied softly.

He shuffled slightly in his chair, his big frame making it creak. 'If I am going too fast, stop me. If I am not making sense or going into things that you don't fully understand, stop me... OK?' he asked.

She nodded and looked back to the muted phone. They both knew they were running out of time.

'Option one sounds too good to be true.' started Cortez, 'They say we can walk, but from my experience, this never comes to fruition. Why leave loose ends that could ultimately come back to bite you in the arse.'

He held her hand tightly now. 'We need more time, we need to plan our next move carefully and we need to be super vigilant. They won't underestimate our capabilities, they will overcompensate. They are professionals and will be expecting us to attempt some sort of trap.'

Genevieve leant forward, 'We stick with our original plan of going to Westminster and The Royal Society to glean more evidence. Upload everything to go viral at the touch of a button.' She chewed her cheek and nodded to her inner monologue. Then she relayed it to Cortez.

'We say we're going with option one, meet somewhere busy, somewhere public, for our protection. But we could live stream the drop, hack the CCTV, we can wear concealed body worn cameras to reveal their identity, use it as insurance?' her mind raced through her plan, she slowed it down to ensure it came out as she thought about it. 'We could then save Sally at the same time. Our terms could be that we hand the case over to them, and we walk out with Sally.'

Cortez nodded in agreement, unmuted the phone and spoke clearly relaying their terms. Then he advised, 'This is when and where we are going to meet.'

*

St. Stephen's Hall, Palace of Westminster, London

The ashen faced redhead shrugged at a confused Massimo, 'I have no idea why Genevieve is so interested in this man?' She looked up at the statue to see if she could grasp something from it but it was hopeless.
Massimo holstered his pistol with an agitated sigh as he began touching the statue, pushing and poking at it to see if he could expose its secrets. But it was solid and gave no clues.
He looked either side of the statue to the beautifully painted frescos adorning the walls. He tapped and knocked at them but they revealed nothing to him. Looking higher still, he examined the stained glass and masonry. But all was consistent with those around the hall.

Then he paused, his eagle eyes had noticed something about the statue.

Looking over his right shoulder to the statue flanking the doorway, he examined the sword in the figure's right hand. Walking back over to the Falkland statue he peered up beneath the crossed palms, and gave a wry smile.
'Tell me Elizabeth, you have worked at Westminster for many years. The other eleven statues are all carved from one piece, correct?' he asked knowingly.

Removing his pocket torch he examined the hands closer still. Climbing up onto the padded green leather bench beside the statue he grasped the bent knee of the Falkland statue pulling himself up so that his eyes were in line with the sword's hilt. He noticed the two scrolled quillons at right angles to the blade and handle. The torch light revealed that the pommel of the cavalry sword was also not secured to the underside of the palms and glove.
Massimo placed his torch into his mouth to free his hands, placing one on each quillon he pulled them downward. Nothing happened. He twisted them back and forth, but again nothing happened.
'Curiouser and curiouser...' He took the torch out of his mouth and licked his lips.

Lifting the sword upward it emitted a low clicking sound. He noticed that the tip of the sword's blade was now an inch out of the statue base.
He slowly pushed the sword back down into the stone as a second click came from within the plinth of the statue. He jumped down and stepped back several paces. A hidden mechanism began to sound, cogs turning and clicking, wheels whirring until the sword dropped into the stone plinth, the hilt now well below the statue's knee with half of the blade now hidden from view.

Massimo and Elizabeth moved closer to inspect the statue. Looking up to where the sword's handle and hilt had been just moments before, now, in its place the tip of a waxed leather tube jutted out. Elizabeth pulled it out, revealing its full length, it was approximately 30 cm by 8 cm. And made from a thick leather dyed dark green and red.

'It is a Roman Capsa, it was designed to transport scrolls such as precious books or important documents in ancient times.' Massimo looked back up to the statue, checking the void that had housed the tube-like Capsa. 'Has anything like this been found here before?' he asked.

Elizabeth shook her head, her eyes transfixed on the ancient scroll case. 'We sometimes find secret passages, or more accurately passages that have been bricked up, boarded up or diverted.' she paused as she fiddled with the fasten clamp, 'But we have never found anything like this.'

'Va bene.' he sniffed, his bruised nose stinging sharply. He snatched the leather tube from Elizabeth by force and shooed her away with a limp hand.

'I can't let you take this.' she protested with futility.

The Italian just looked at her in amazement. He couldn't believe the audacity of this young woman.

'We have to process this, open it up and see what is inside.' she continued adamantly, still trying to take the Capsa back from him.

The doors beside them flew open making them both spin. Cortez and Genevieve were being escorted through the hall by two armed police officers. On seeing the Italian Cortez moved in front of Genevieve creating a human shield, he picked her up and pushed her back through to the connecting hall. He raised a hand pointing towards Massimo, 'Armed and extremely dangerous!' he shouted as the two armed officers raised their assault rifles in unison, both trained on the Italian's head.

'Drop the tube and raise your hands, right now!' one of them shouted. Massimo was in no position to argue. He carefully dropped the ancient Capsa tube onto the tiled floor and raised both gloved hands, causing his suit jacket to open revealing his pistol holstered beneath his armpit. On seeing this the other police officer moved in closer, 'Elizabeth move behind us and out of the door, now!'

Elizabeth grabbed the discarded Capsa and sprinted out of the hall towards Cortez and Genevieve.
The Italian stood in silence as he watched Cortez, Genevieve, Elizabeth and more importantly the mysterious Capsa disappear through the doors at the other end of the building. 'Gentlemen, can we talk about this?' he asked diffidently as the two officers moved in on him. One placed a hand on his chest mounted radio to call through for backup as the other came in close to remove Massimo's pistol. 'English police are renowned for their hospitality,' he smiled as he spoke, 'But as we are in the house of politicians, how about some corruption? How about £100,000 each if you let me walk out of here right now?'

He raised an eyebrow as they exchanged a quick glance. He took in every detail as he spoke, their height, weight, handedness, weapons, exposed skin and anything that he could use to his advantage.

Their radios crackled into life as one looked down to his chest to reply. Massimo seized the moment and leapt into action. Placing one gloved hand on the nearest officer's exposed neck, paralysing him instantly, he removed the stunned officer's own pistol from his leg holster and used it on the second distracted officer who was momentarily preoccupied with his radio, he glanced up as two consecutive rounds thudded into his head.

Massimo moved his gloved hand away as the first officer fell heavily to the ground. Foam emitting from his mouth. He promptly disconnected the security lanyard from the base of the dead officer's pistol grip and collected his own pistol before standing upright, he brushed himself down. The two radios cackled in unison as urgent messages relayed back and forth, the voices frantic. He considered confiscating one of the chattering radios but knew that as soon as the bodies were found the access code and frequency channel would be changed making them useless to him. Besides, he had wasted too much time already. "Carpe Diem" he muttered to himself as he ran through the hall after Genevieve and Cortez.

*

Genevieve chanced a glance behind her as she saw six armed officers running in the opposite direction, she only then realised that she had been holding Cortez's hand since they had started running. She loosened her grip to see bloodied nail marks in the back of his large hand. 'I am so sorry.' she exclaimed in shock.

Cortez just smiled back, he looked down at his hand but appeared not to have even noticed the four scarlet crescents until she had mentioned them.
'This way!' shouted Elizabeth as she led them down corridors and through doorways usually closed to the general public. She pushed the small red box beside the door as a penetrating klaxon reverberated throughout Westminster. Once they were inside a large meeting room she locked the door behind them. 'Who the hell was that man Genevieve?' Elizabeth spat, as she tried to stop her hands from shaking violently.

'He is a hitman who has been hired to kill us and take back these scroll fragments written two thousand years ago by a Roman surveyor to his employer.' started Genevieve raising the case in her hand, pausing when she saw the ancient leather tube in Elizabeth's shaking hands. 'What is that?'

Controlling her breath she replied, 'This was hidden inside that statue, the one you wanted to see.' Her eyes were very suspicious of her old friend. 'What on earth is going on here Genevieve?' She asked earnestly.
Genevieve and Cortez looked at each other, 'The Claudius Scrolls! So Flint was telling the truth.' started Cortez moving in closer. 'Have you opened it?' He asked her as he examined the old dry leather casing.
She shook her head, then looked back to the locked door as two gunshots echoed through the building. All three of them remained deathly silent, waiting to hear something from outside. Eyes transfixed on the locked door.

Cortez scanned the room and made for the small window. The thin metal frames had been painted shut over the years and he didn't like the idea of breaking the entire window of a listed building. But as sounds of shouting and screams filled the corridors outside he thought better on what the priority was here. Grabbing the nearby wooden chair he threw it through the myriad of small glass panes as the entire frame buckled and fell outwards.
'Come on!' he shouted, waving the two ladies through the now open window. Once they were all out of the building Cortez looked up behind him to see the towering iconic landmark of Big Ben standing directly above them. He turned to Elizabeth and Genevieve only to see they had already sprinted across New Palace Yard and were now heading across the street into Parliament Square.

He exclaimed as he chased after them. The area was now swarming with armed response vehicles and several military personnel stationed within Parliament. The closest Police officers instructed the three of them to run directly to a cordoned area. Genevieve could now see Parliament members, staff and tourists were all being evacuated from the main buildings. It was a scene of pure chaos.

Once they had ducked the police tape and rounded several corners they found themselves in the expanse that was St James Park. Other than pigeons and squirrels the park was mostly deserted. Genevieve explained all to her old friend with details of everything that had transpired and why the Italian hitman had been waiting for them in St. Stephen's Hall. They ran past the dark lake and up through the pathways leading to the public café. It was busier here with people sitting on the benches, dog walkers, runners and families. All seemed so tranquil and calm. But for the three of them they knew there was still the risk that they were being hunted by a highly-trained murderer. And they were running out of time.

Making their way across The Mall they arrived outside the Royal Society's main building. The frontage was simplistic, in a neo-classic design. The dark windows were framed with bold, clean and neat columns, all coated with an abundance of white paint. The tiered steps that led up toward the towering Duke of York monument were occupied by a primary school group enjoying their packed lunches.
Carlton House Terrace was bustling with works vans, lorries and vehicles parked opposite the main entrance.

'We don't have much time so we have to work fast,' he said assuredly as they rounded the corner. Glancing down he could see the building's basement service door.

'We should split up, try to cover more ground.' Having decided to attempt the basement's service door, he hurdled the black iron gate and railings and descended the curving steps until he was picking the old lock as Genevieve and Elizabeth kept watch from above. Within seconds he was inside and was closing the door behind him. The two then carried on the short distance further along Carlton House Terrace until they were outside the entrance proper, set back from the road. They were to attempt to access the vaults by sheer chance and kind persuasion. Either way they had to succeed.

Genevieve and Elizabeth walked through the main door to be met by two younger men at the reception. A flash of her Parliament I.D. badge and Elizabeth had the two men fully attentive to what she was saying within seconds. She fed them a convincing white lie that was suspiciously plausible and feasible. She was a natural liar. A trait picked up from working with politicians all day.

She explained how Parliament had wanted to host a new exhibition featuring the works of the old masters, one of them being Sir Christopher Wren. She had come with her historical conservation liaison officer, Genevieve, to examine the plans, sketches and illustration plates held within the vault at the Royal Society to see what would suffice for the exhibition. The two young men looked impressed and eager to assist, but when they insisted on calling *upstairs* for approval on access and for someone to arrange a meeting some weeks down the line.

Genevieve stepped up with her decisive and assertive fictitious character role. Playing the part of bad cop a bit too well.

Her eyes flitted to the Latin inscription emblazoned on the wall behind the two men, *"Nullius in verba"*, which translates as, 'Take nobody's word for it'. She half smiled at the irony of their current situation.

The two young men feeling suitably abashed they succumbed and allowed access into the vault, as long as they were escorted. Genevieve excitedly squeezed Elizabeth's arm gently as they took their security lanyards, placing them around their necks. At the end of the stylish corridor decorated in paintings, maps and copious green pot plants they came to the large elevator.

It opened with a metallic ping as an automated voice announced the floor level.

Stepping inside they were met by a large, thick-necked asian male with a shaved head and thin goatee beard. His fierce demeanour dropped as he exchanged a smile with the two ladies. 'Which floor?' he asked. His accent was that of Lancashire or the north.

'Not seen you two before.' he asked openly, his large attentive brown eyes hastily swept over them from head to toe, then lingered on their security lanyards.

Elizabeth answered, relaying the same story as she had told the two receptionists that they were from Parliament and needed to assess the workings of Wren. The large man tapped the letter "B" and swiped his own lanyard over the wall mounted sensor sending the row of three yellow LEDs to green before the lift doors closed and it began its brief descent. 'Go left and through the double doors, then take a right. You will see the sign for the vault at the end of the long corridor.' he chirped as the elevator came to a gentle stop and the doors opened making the same metallic ting and the automated voice announced, "Basement".

Following the instructions given to them they arrived at the security doors of the Royal Society's main vault. The large door and frame was constructed of what looked like stained wood but on closer inspection it was reinforced titanium metal. Genevieve sent a brief text message to Cortez who was somewhere inside the building. He replied immediately with a link and a second message that simply read, "Press me". Genevieve did as instructed and her phone became a close range tracker and microphone.

Elizabeth leant forward scanning her lanyard on the wall mounted sensor, but nothing happened. She tried again, with the same result. They exchanged a panicked look as Genevieve stepped forward to try her lanyard. This was when she recalled Flint mentioning the Biometric security system. "Shit." she thought to herself.

'You will need a special keycard to open that door.' came a female voice from behind them. They turned to find a tall, smartly dressed lady standing in the corridor. She wore a tanned leather jacket, black vest top and green cargo trousers. 'The boys upstairs called down stating that they needed security to escort two ladies inside the vaults.' she smiled at them.

'I am Penny, Head of Governance and Compliance at the Royal Society. I wrote my dissertation on Wren so I thought I would be an asset for your exhibition, or should you have any questions.' Stepping forward she tapped the sensor as the large wood-effect door swung open silently. 'The Biometric system is down again.' She smiled tapping a small scanner to the right of the door. Through the door was a small antichamber made of glass and thin metal framing. Once inside it the main door closed behind them, a rush of cold air then ruffled their hair as the door on the opposite side of the chamber opened. 'Air lock.' answered Penny rhetorically as the two ladies looked at her nonplussed. 'Keeps everything inside safe from fire, damp and pests.'

Inside the vaults were rows of high-density mobile shelving storage systems on floor tracks that could be moved by simply spinning a wheel to create an aisle only where needed to maximise space. Along the centre of the large room were modern solid wooden desks similar to those used by architects, each desk was accompanied by comfortable wheelie chairs.

'Not what I was expecting.' mouthed Genevieve as she took it all in.

'When the Royal Society was moved here in 1967 from Burlington House, they ensured advancements were made. We pride ourselves on being very progressive, ensuring the most state-of-the-art and contemporary technologies are used.' Replied Penny matter-of-factly. 'Apart from the Biometric system, that is always breaking so we hardly use it anymore.'

The modern finishes were far from the traditional static shelving that she was used to seeing in museum vaults. The ceilings were dotted with what looked like a two dimensional christmas tree of blinking LEDs for the multiple temperature and moisture sensors and fire and smoke detectors. The bright lighting ensured no dark areas or shadows were present making viewing the ancient documents enclosed within the shelving easier.

'So,' asked Penny, 'What sort of thing are you looking for for this special exhibition?'

'We are looking for Wren's plans and sketches of the original foundations of St. Paul's,' said Genevieve hopefully. Penny looked at her intently before half smiling, she tapped a tablet on a nearby desk making the screen light up.

'When the Great Fire of London destroyed most of the mediaeval buildings, Christopher Wren submitted plans to rebuild the majority of those destroyed buildings. Not many know that his plans were actually rejected at first.' Penny tapped away until a series of numbers and digits appeared on the screen. 'Here we are,' she walked across to the high-density mobile shelving storage systems and matched up the numbers from the tablet. 'This one.' she smiled broadly. Spinning the three armed ergonomic handles the storage cabinets parted silently revealing rows of shelves stacked with files, folders and boxes. Penny walked into the now wide aisle and up to the section she was looking for. She pulled out a large folder and carried it back out to the desk where the tablet was placed. Genevieve and Elizabeth stood either side of her as she opened the file.

'These are the letters written between Christopher Wren and Sir Issac Newton following the Great Fire.' she pulled out a smaller box and handed it to Genevieve, she then took out a second larger file and handed it to Elizabeth. 'And these are Wren's writings on what he found beneath the rubble.' She paused for a moment, as though thinking her next move through before she carried it out. Stepping back she folded her arms, a frown covered her beautiful face, 'You mentioned the "original" foundations.' She eyed them closely. 'I am not going to assume what you know, nor am I going to ask how you know what you may, or may not know.' She leant in and opened the first folder. 'These letters of correspondence detail the structures found beneath the ashes and charred timbers, I studied them all for my dissertation on Wren. They reveal things that have been described as nonsensical and fantastical by the academia of old. And scrutinised and challenged by the Church for centuries.'

'Penny, we know about the Goddess Path Temple.' admitted Genevieve. 'We know that after the great fire of 1666, all the charred building remains were levelled revealing the ruins of the Roman temple beneath St. Paul's. We know that the site was used for ceremonial rituals long before the Romans arrived. We just need to see the documents for ourselves.'

Penny opened the second box containing Wren's original sketches and detailed reports. 'Everything you need is inside this box.' Her hands shook with a combination of anticipation and excitement as she laid out the three hundred and fifty year old drawings atop the wooden desk. 'I have been wanting to talk to someone about this for nearly five years.' she beamed with excitement. 'It has been hidden for too long.'

'Tell her Genevieve.' said Elizabeth flatly with an eyebrow raised.

Genevieve stood silent, biting her bottom lip as she always did when lost in thought. How could she tell this stranger what had happened, and what they needed to do, knowing that Sally's life was still at risk if they didn't comply. She steeled herself then opened her mouth, to reveal all and seek the aid of this stranger. 'So, you have heard of the Goddess-'

'Penelope?!' interrupted a mordant faced man in a tweed suit from behind them. 'What is going on here?' he asked irritably as he approached the three of them. 'Who are these two?' he spat pointing his finger at them.

'I am Elizabeth Tanner from the Palace of Westminister and Parliament,' she started, taking out her I.D. badge to show the tweed man. 'And this is-'

'I know full well who she is, Genevieve Silankis.' His face puckered as if he were eating a ridiculously sour fruit. 'Treasure hunter and hack.' he spat. 'You should not be in here.' he pointed his finger at her chest menacingly.

'I am not a treasure hunter or a hack, thank you very much.' she retorted indignantly.

'Penelope, explain yourself.' he ordered. His sharp narrow eyes looked down at the documents laid upon the table. On seeing Wren's documents he began shaking his head. 'No!' he called. 'This is outrageous Penelope!' he boomed. 'This ridiculous conspiracy has gone too far. I warned you about this.'

'But, Lord Crane, it is not a simple conspiracy, there is so much evidence that if you would only allow me to show you...' The tweed man just held up his hand to her face.

'Enough!' he shouted. 'All three of you will leave this facility and building at once.'

Penelope's eyes welled up, she shook her head in disbelief. She turned to the two ladies opening her mouth, but no words came out.

'If you had to,' started Genevieve to Penny, 'would you sacrifice something extremely important for the pursuit of knowledge? To ensure truth will out?' Penny nodded back firmly, drying her red eyes with her leather jacket sleeve.

Genevieve simply smiled back at her. 'Now Cortez.' she said softly as the room plunged into darkness. The flashing LEDs above them resembled a multicoloured constellation flickering in the dark night sky. The security door at the far end of the room opened revealing the silhouette of a large figure in the rays of the outer hallway's bright light. The figure ran inside the air chamber as the door closed behind them as all returned to darkness. The sound of the second air-lock door swooshed open in the abyss.

'Penny, take my hand.' called Genevieve into the darkness. 'Lizzy, hold on.'

They could hear rummaging on the tables in front of them, the sound of papers being rustled, tidied and tapped together on the table.

'Penelope! Explain yourself. What the devil is going on here?!' Spat tweed man desperately.

Genevieve, Elizabeth and Penny were escorted blindly across the room, linked by hands held like young children moving as one through a busy museum on a school trip.

The air-lock security door opened and closed once again as tweed man watched the large silhouette leave followed by three much smaller figures. The main door closed as darkness entombed him. 'Hello?' he called out, but all was silent in the blackness.

*

West Cloister, House of Commons, London

Massimo launched himself against a wood panelled wall, his chest tight, both from exertion and from the multiple rounds that he had taken in the chest and back as he moved his way through Parliament. His bespoke tailored Kevlar suit now resembled a polka dot pattern.

Taking several deep breaths in he paused his mind. Exhaling heavily he focused his eyes on his destination. The ornate masonry of the fire exit at the end of the West Cloister corridor. He stepped out, pistol raised and ready, taking several large strides forward as four heavily armoured men in multi-terrain pattern (MTP) combat clothing with Osprey assault body armour came around the opposite end of the corridor directly in front of the fire exit door. He cursed and ducked back against the wood panelled wall for some cover as they continued their hasty approach. He was no match for their SA80 A2s or body armour.

He noticed a small brass key-hole on the wall next to his head. He tapped it as the wood panel opened up swinging outward revealing a small stone-floored chamber behind. He didn't hesitate as he jumped through it. He inspected the room, old graffiti was scrawled along some of the walls, to the far wall he could see a bricked-up doorway.

Several heavy kicks later the ancient bricks fell to the floor as he peered through to Westminster Hall. He dislodged several more bricks to make a hole large enough for him to squeeze through as two flash bangs came tinkling into the small chamber by his feet.

These were followed by a smoking canister of tear gas. He clenched his eyes closed and flopped out the other side as the thick choking smoke funnelled out of his small hole and he sprinted, teary eyed across the hall back to the passage he had entered the building through earlier that morning, back to Westminster Abbey.

Massimo had followed his earlier footsteps back to the Cellarium Cafe as he collapsed in the deserted kitchen. He pushed open the small window and felt the cool gentle breeze on his face, the tear gas had naturally made his nose tickle and eyes water. He opened one of the kitchen's large food prep taps, holding his head under the water for as long as he could, flushing out the nerve agents from his eyes, nose and throat. The effects were now no worse than Hayfever. He had never suffered from Hayfever in his youth, but for some reason England in early summer always made him react. He downed some more antihistamine tablets and strong pain killers and rubbed his nose regretting it instantly. Cortez's fists had done a real number on his face, his nose was certainly broken and the tear gas had inflamed the tissue causing his entire face to ache in agony.

His phone chirped from the sideboard beside him, he flipped it over and opened his covert location App. A map opened up showing the East of England, it slowly zoomed in to show Colchester. A small crosshair appeared over the castle and started blinking. 'Va bene' he muttered as he stood up. Checking his watch he rolled his eyes gesturing a prayer with his hands. 'Three hours remaining. Tempus fugit.'

He had to get out of London as soon as possible, with all agencies on highest alert this was definitely not the place for a professional hitman to linger.

*

Pall Mall, London

Genevieve hailed a passing taxi outside of The Travellers Club as they jumped into the back, 'Liverpool Street Station, quick as you can please.' she ordered through the perspex screen. 'You'll be lucky love,' replied the stalwart cabbie, 'Traffic is mental at the minute. Underground has been closed and everything is at a standstill.'
Cortez slapped two crisp red £50 notes with the face of Alan Turing onto the dividing screen, making the driver look over his shoulder. 'This is yours if you can get us there.'
The cabbie cricked his neck, and muttered to himself but took the notes and pulled away into the slow moving traffic.

Penny looked over her shoulder, half expecting someone to be chasing after them. But nobody did. She turned back to the three others in the back of the Hackney. 'What just happened?' she asked in disbelief.
Cortez leant forward stretching out his large hand, 'Name's Cortez, pleasure to meet you.' he smiled. He went on to explain how he had been hidden away within the belly of the Royal Society building listening in to their conversation via Genny's mobile. How he had killed the security system and cameras, then the lighting before extracting the three of them and the Wren documents under cover of darkness before they all made a dash for the nearest taxi.

Genevieve explained about what had happened to them, to Sally and the people that had taken her. About how these mysterious people want all documentation and records of the ancient Goddess Path and its associated temples destroyed from all existence.

'I think I have had dealings with these people before.' started Penny knowingly.

'You're Flint's inside man?' asked Cortez. His intelligent eyes watched her intently.

She nodded silently in response. Then she spoke, 'When I wrote my dissertation on Wren, I uncovered notes on the ruins beneath St. Pauls. I began finding coincidences in other documents and the letters between Wren and Newton. That is when Flint made contact. He had the same beliefs as me, but we searched too deeply and disturbed the unwanted attention of the ancient Order of the Sun or *Ordo Solis*.'

'Just like the Balrog in Moria.' muttered Cortez, shaking his head.

'I was instructed, well actually I was made to drop everything by the Executive Director of the Royal Society. She said it was for my own safety, but she wouldn't explain. Then Lord Crane threatened my career at the Society if I spoke out about it. Then he had Flint banned from coming to Carlton House Terrace, I was completely isolated. And I kept my mouth shut and nose clean. All of my hard work had been rejected as conspiracy and discredited as inadmissible for my dissertation. I had almost forgotten about it until this morning when I heard from Flint out of the blue about you Genevieve.' she said looking across the taxi to her. 'So I made sure I was the one who would meet you and escort you inside the vault.'

'We need to travel to Colchester to save my friend Sally Thorgood.' started Cortez. 'She is only safe if we hand over everything associated with the Goddess Path that we have managed to gather. We have the Roman surveyor Antonius Pietra fragments, the Claudius Scrolls and now we have the Wren manuscripts and plates.'

'But you cannot just hand them over to these people!' screamed Penny, 'Too much knowledge has been lost to these people already. For too long the truth has been hidden. Rewritten by these ideological terrorists to promote their lies.'

'You sound just like Flint.' smiled Cortez warmly.

'That is exactly why we have been making copies.' smiled Genevieve reassuringly. 'It is our insurance policy.'

Genevieve took out her mobile and began recording their every movement, Elizabeth nodded and opened the ancient leather Capsa, tipping it on an angle to dislodge the contents. Two tightly rolled scrolls slid out into her lap.
The two scrolls were bound around two slim wooden pegs, each capped with rounded ornate stained wooden knobs that resembled cabinet door handles.
They were fastened with a leather strap and bore the red disc of sealing wax. The seal had been partially broken in places but the marking was still clear.

Genevieve read it out as she moved the mobile camera closer, 'TI CLAVDIVS CAESAR AVG P M TRP IMP PP'
Elizabeth nodded, 'That is the seal of Tiberius Claudius Caesar Augustus P M TRP Imperator Pater Patriae.'
'What's that then?' asked the cabbie inquisitively peering back at them through his mirror as the four of them leant in over the ancient priceless scrolls.

Cortez coughed awkwardly but shrugged his shoulders and let loose. 'It's a two thousand year old handwritten scroll penned by Emperor Claudius detailing a secret network of pagan ritual stone pathways that he traversed on a clandestine quest in 43 AD. The pathways ran across ancient England but all knowledge of it has been purged and hidden by the Catholic Church. We are on a time-sensitive mission to save my friend, stop a crazed European hitman and bring down one of the world's most powerful religious organisations.'

'Oh yeah?' pouted the cabbie, unconcerned by what had just been disclosed to him, 'You know that Claudius faked his own death to escape his successor Nero and moved to a luxury villa in Pompeii with his lover and servant and lived happily until the fated eruption of 79 AD.' replied the cabbie matter-of-factly.

'Ha!' laughed Cortez, 'My man.' he chuckled to himself.

'Stop!' called Elizabeth as Genevieve was about to break the two thousand year old wax seal. 'This should be conducted under the correct environment.' She said looking at the state and condition of the floor and seats of the taxi. 'This is far from sterile.' she whispered, not wanting to offend the driver.

'We need to go back to the University of Essex Colchester Campus.' replied Cortez with a hesitant look toward Genevieve.

They stopped outside Liverpool Street Station as the cabbie unlocked the doors allowing them to alight. Cortez stepped out first, his experienced eyes looking for anything untoward. Anything out of place, anyone watching them. Once he was happy that they hadn't been followed he ushered the others out onto the busy sidewalk.

The central head house and concourse was swarming with passengers moving in every direction. Like scurrying ants across the jungle floor. High above them suspended from the Victorian engineered high collumned steel and glass ceiling sat the ever changing departure board. The twenty one orange columns of digital text flitted as trains departed, updated and replaced with future journeys.

Genevieve's eyes ran across the Departures board until she saw what they were after. 'Platform 11,' she called as they sprinted across the station. 'We should arrive in 58 minutes.' she called over her shoulder as they arrived at the platform. Cortez and Elizabeth checked their watches as they climbed aboard the huge white, red and yellow Greater Anglia train sat ready to disembark to Colchester.

*

Driving the dead Antiquities Dealer's car through East London, Massimo made quick progress along the A12. He'd ensured the new registration plates wouldn't attract any attention. Having taken it from a vehicle of the same make, colour and model. He tapped the steering wheel anxiously as he approached Colchester's historic town centre. He only had two hours to finalise the mission or he himself would be a deadman.

This time of the day both vehicle and foot traffic was always quiet. After a brisk walk around the castle and its surrounding parkland he found the perfect elevated location to oversee the drop off. 'Always take the higher ground,' he said to no one as he began his ascent to the top of the north east tower of the ancient castle. 'Now we wait.' he smirked as he looked through the scope of his L115A3 long-range sniper rifle across Mayors Walk, through the trees down the grass bank to the Band Stand below.

*

Chapter 10
Campus & Castles

Colchester University

The train journey had allowed enough time for Genevieve to update Flint and Nicola Stirling respectively. They had both been curious as to her next steps, but she ensured that only she and Cortez knew their ultimate plan.

The walk back into the University had been difficult for Genevieve, it had not even been twenty-four hours since she was held at gunpoint, but she could still see and hear the harsh raspy accented voice and final words of Armon Di Silva the Arms Dealer. No matter how much she tried, her busy mind stubbornly showed her the replay of his lifeless body hitting the ground in slow motion. She snapped out of her thoughts as she realised they had now entered the corridor in which she had fallen. She looked down to the polished floor where she had lain, it was spotless. The door and surrounding frame had been replaced and redecorated after Massimo had kicked it from its hinges.

She braved a glimpse inside to see the furniture and desks had been removed and the old floor had been ripped up, two balding men in tattered knee padded denim jeans and matching polo shirts looked up at her from on all fours. They were busily trowelling a thick grey self levelling screed over the exposed concrete. She could see the section where Armon had fallen, even with the flooring removed the distinct stain of dark red marked the concrete below. Her mind replayed the scene once more as she felt her stomach lurch, coldness filled her insides.

Cortez placed an arm around her moving her along the corridor, 'Come on Dove,' he said softly. 'Let's keep moving eh.' He half looked inside as he walked her along the corridor. And just like that the screed was laid over the blood spatter stain removing it from existence. By tomorrow there would be no remnants of what had transpired within that room. "Ignorance is bliss" he thought as they walked back to the laboratory floors.

The white coated youthful technicians looked sheepishly between themselves as the four of them walked into their lab. 'The whole place has been talking...' started Beth hesitantly. Standing up to meet them. 'What the hell happened?' she asked as two of the technicians looked as though they were about to leave, possibly to call security. That was until they saw Genevieve pull out the ancient scroll from its leather Capsa. 'We need your help.' she looked up at them, half baiting them with the promise of an ancient scroll. 'It belonged to Emperor Claudius.' One sat down immediately, her eyes wide. The other rolled their eyes, huffed indignantly then returned to their station with folded arms.
Cortez asked them to assist with the examination of the two-thousand-year-old scroll. Within twenty minutes they had high-definition digital scans of both sides of the document. And an advanced translation of the text from Latin to modern English. Genevieve, Elizabeth and Penny stood around the printout as Genevieve read it aloud as Cortez recorded it on his mobile. Once she had finished the room stood in absolute silence.
'Oh, my goodness.' gasped Elizabeth loudly, her hands over her mouth. 'This is huge!' She smiled.

'Beth,' asked Cortez to the lab technician, 'Any chance we could borrow your car?'
The young lab technician looked awkwardly at her colleagues before shrugging.

'The central locking mechanism is broken so you have to use the key on each door but help yourselves. I guess.'

*

Cortez pulled over to park on Ryegate Road next to a seven foot red brick wall that encircled most of the castle's parkland. He placed his hand on Genevieve's thigh, giving it a gentle squeeze. She turned, holding his gaze. Penny and Elizabeth clambered out and began to walk the perimeter of the garden wall up to the nearest opening.

'You ready for this Genny?' he asked, keeping his eyes forward, scanning the empty streets around them. 'There is an hour before we meet them inside.' he said, nodding over to the bandstand.

Genevieve opened the Samsonite case checking everything was inside. She closed it and nodded. More to assert herself than anything. She felt viciously nauseous and had to focus on her breathing to attempt to slow her thumping heart from breaking through her tight chest.

'You remember the plan?' he asked her for the twentieth time. She remained silent, biting her cheek. She nodded assertively then unclipped her seatbelt.

'I am going to sweep the castle and check the perimeter of the park.' he said with a sedated self possession. 'Then I will come and meet you at the bandstand where we will wait for our mysterious guests.'

'Simon. If anything happens to Sally, I wouldn't know what to-' started Genevieve desperately.

Cortez just raised his hand, placing a large finger on her soft pink lips. 'Shh now Genny.' he whispered. 'Everything is going to be ok. Trust me.' he forced out a smile. 'Now wait here until it's time, then walk through to the bandstand. I'll see you there in thirty minutes,'

He clambered out of their borrowed car, it was far too small for him but he managed eventually. The road was empty, save for a few local resident's cars further up the road. He walked at pace to the opening, thirty yards up from where he had parked and entered the lush green expanse of the Colchester Castle landscaped gardens. The castle proper was up on the hill to his right and to his left, he could just see the tip of the bandstand through the colourful flower beds and boulevard of tall trees.

The gardens were masterfully landscaped around the stone footprints of the Roman foundations, showing the footings of the ancient buildings that once stood in this beautiful area. With lush green lawns, bountiful flower beds and rows of well managed trees. The sun shone above, a change from the recent wet weather that had brought out scores of local residents intent on making the most of the summer sun. Families walked, children screamed and played in excitement, couples talked, dogs were pulling their keepers along and people cycled along.

Cortez made light work of the perimeter check and was now making his way up the sloped parterre enclosed either side by hedges and colourful flower beds. Jogging up to the castle, he paused taking in the high defensive walls, the arrow holes, then along to the small structure atop the corner tower topped with a radio transmission aerial.

Its window opened causing him to double take on it. He instinctively moved to his right taking cover behind one of the large trees. Although he was still a good forty metres away and it was dark in the window frame, he was certain that he recognised it as the bruised face of Massimo.

Cortez swore under his breath. From the elevated position the Italian could see everything, including him if he were to move out from behind the tree. He was stuck and time was running out. He needed to distract the Italian and fast. His mind raced for inspiration, tapping his pockets he felt his phone, a pocket knife and some wire cutters. Grabbing his backpack he tore it open and smiled. 'Thank you Genny.' He grinned. Genevieve had purchased him a miniature remote control drone for his birthday the previous month, which true to his form, he had instantly dismantled it and modified the tech. Now fully enhanced and operational he placed it on the ground and took out his mobile. The LEDs flashed from green to red and the four blades began to spin silently in unison. He glanced back up to the window to see the tip of a rifle barrel rest on the window ledge above.
'Shit just got real' he muttered to himself.
Piloting the stealth drone through his phone it rose up higher than the castle and circled the north eastern tower just above the radio transmission aerial.

Timing would be crucial for his plan to work, he had to distract the Italian long enough for him to get clear of his line of sight. This meant running twenty metres in four seconds. The drone descended to the window on the far side, furthest away from Cortez and to the right of where Massimo now perched high up in his snipers nest. Cortez drove the drone hard into the closed window causing one of the small squares of glass to crack. The sudden unexpected thud sound had done exactly what he had hoped.

From within the top of the tower Massimo flinched, his head snapped to the right, away from the resting sniper scope to inspect what had caused this unexpected noise. On seeing the now cracked small square pane of glass he moved over to see what had been the cause. On seeing nothing outside he assumed it was a passing bird, knowing that they were incapable of seeing glass and often collided with window panes, especially at this height. His eyes flitted cautiously back to the rifle at the other window and he resumed his position. "Something didn't feel right" He thought as he tightened his grip on the rifle.

As soon as the drone had hit the far window Cortez had lifted the drone high above the castle. At the same time he had sprinted across the clearing from his hiding place to the north west corner of the castle and past the rows of benches and waste bins that lined the pathway surrounding the castle base. The drone landed silently in front of him as he scooped it up, throwing it back into his backpack.

He entered the castle and ran to the north eastern tower. Pocket knife in hand he pressed his ear against the closed door. It was almost impossible to hear anything inside, but then he heard Massimo talking to himself.
"Lei arriva." he heard from inside the room. "ma è sola." Cortez couldn't hear a second voice and was unsure if the Italian was alone, but he had to risk that he was. He checked his watch, so much time had already passed. "Genny." he thought. There was no time to waste, he couldn't allow Genevieve to be at risk of this psychopath.

He kicked the oak door open and stormed inside, knife raised and ready to take out the hitman. But the rifle was unoccupied. Cortez had hoped that Massimo would have had his back to the door, but he had somehow known or expected someone was outside the door.

Cortez felt the boot before he could see anything, his right knee screamed in agony as he fell to the ground. Massimo had been waiting just inside the door pressed against the wall, ready to pounce. And pounce he did.

Cortez released a heavy back hand from his lowered position, but the trained Italian blocked it easily. Countering with a heavy left punch to Cortez's cheek sending him flat to the ground. The hitman walked around him, now between Cortez and the door and the open window behind him.

Cortez pushed himself up, his eyes cold, his demeanour pissed.

The Italian folded his arms and smiled. 'Just a little thank you for the last time we met.' he said pointing to his bruised face and busted nose.

Cortez rubbed his cheek but said nothing. Rolling his large shoulders back he raised the pocket knife and took a step forward.

'Così comincia.' sneered the Italian. He removed his Sig Sauer P320 with its custom suppressor and laid it on the table beside him. 'We are both men of honour, let us fight man to man.' he smiled, pulling a serrated blade from a concealed holster on his lower back.

It had been years since Cortez had used a knife in hand to hand combat, but it was training that stuck with you. Like riding a bike, but deadlier. The two of them circled the compact room, their eyes locked, their stances almost identical. One hand raised, gripping their respective knife handle, the other raised with open palm like a Karate chop.

Blow after blow their blades struck, the speed was sensational. Blurs of silver were exchanged between the two of them. The sound emitted was more that of a metallic scraping than the *ting ting* that was heard in swashbuckling or 80's action movies.

The Italian's style and technique was textbook, crisp, powerful, and focused. Like a well rehearsed kata the inherent pattern of actions were sickeningly accurate. Cortez had been fighting since he was a child, both on and off the streets of London. Trouble with a local gang had resulted in him taking up boxing, then martial arts. It wasn't long before the gangs gave him a wide berth. That was before he had joined the military. His polymath mind combined with his physical strength, speed, or endurance made him a perfect weapon.

Cortez saw an opening and moved in closer, grabbing the Italian by the elbow he forced his blade in hard under a wide attack. It hit the target but didn't penetrate. He looked down in disbelief as the Italian just smiled back. 'Like my father used to say, always use protection. You didn't think I would come to a fight without protection?' he laughed mockingly, pushing Cortez back he released a vicious jab followed by a cross that sent Cortez against the wall. Cortez unleashed several high kicks sending the Italian back several paces. Then followed through with a heavy stomach punch, connecting with all his might. Massimo doubled and swore loudly. 'Vaffanculo!!' he spat on the ground but regained his composure instantly. His diaphragm already bruised from the baseball bat, this winded him something terrible. He needed a second to catch his breath.

'You are good Cortez. I am still trying to figure you out.' He watched the larger man switch his knife hold as he readied himself for another bout. He had experienced combat with dozens of soldiers, special forces and other professional hitmen. But Cortez had a unique style. Sloppy in comparison yet still extremely effective, and dangerous.

'Your proletariat technique is questionable.' laughed Massimo, allowing a light snigger. 'Gutter fighting at its best.' Cortez saw red. He hated one thing more than anything else. Classist snobs demeaning and degrading him because of his background.

'Seems effective enough you blue-blooded prick.' retorted Cortez. 'I had to put up with enough of you *figlio di papà* when I was bodyguarding in Sardinia.' He unleashed a vicious slicing backhand that Massimo narrowly avoided, the top of his shirt tore slightly but again no blood was drawn. Had he not moved back the blade would have made contact with his throat. He laughed aloud, 'That was close.' he said in a timorous voice. Unbeknownst to Cortez, his pithy comment of calling him *figlio di papà* had caught him off guard. His mind flashed instantly back to the children in Italy decades before who had taunted and bullied him for his aristocratic lifestyle. The life he had tried so hard to escape.

He calmed his breathing, focused on his opponent, they were equally matched with a blade. It was time to try something else. The most effective weapon you have, other than your mind, is the weapon your enemy doesn't know you have.

'This suit has several secrets,' started the Hitman, his mind now fully back in the present. Focused, charged and attentive. He spoke softly, slipping on his specialist gloves. 'Not only is it Kevlar lined, it has another design feature of my own creation. Have you heard of Faraday?' he asked as he walked in closer to a hesitant Cortez. 'It is designed to block electromagnetic fields.' he said as he brushed his jacket down with his gloved hands, regaining his suave, sophisticated composure. 'But what makes it more spectacular is that I can harness up to 250,000 volts at my fingertips.' he lurched forward with shocking speed knocking Cortez's defensive blows away and placed his hands on Cortez's exposed bearded neck. Cortez gasped, his breath agonal as he shot back, bolt upright against the wall, his teeth grinding together. 'Let's see how much you can take, tough guy.' smiled the hitman tightening his grip choking Cortez.

*

Genevieve had done as instructed. She walked alone through the avenue of trees to the central bandstand, the Samsonite case in one hand and the Capsa over her shoulder. Standing alone she nervously looked around her for Cortez.

'Where are you Cortez?' she asked herself. She tried his phone for the tenth time as it rang off to his answer message.

'Miss Silankis?' asked a suited man from behind her. She jumped at his unexpected presence. He wore a fine suit and a small circular pin on his lapel, crossed-keys within a sun.

'Ordo Solis.' she mouthed quietly to herself.

She turned to see two other men now standing there, Sally was between them. Her hands were bound and Genevieve could just make out that she had a strip of clear heavy-duty tape across her mouth. Clear tape was much less conspicuous than manhandling a duct taped woman around a public park. From a distance nothing could be seen.

'Where is Mr Lewes? Or *Cortez* as you call him.' asked the first suited man. Looking around the busy parkland. He was tall, middle-aged and completely emotionless. His demeanour was more robot than human.

'The deal was both of you with all the documents.' Spoke another of the suited men.

'He will be here.' replied Genevieve anxiously, also looking around for her friend.

'If you are planning some sort of mischievous ploy,' started the last suited man. His accent was unmistakably european. 'We will kill you.' he pulled open his jacket to expose the butt of a pistol beneath his armpit.

'He is on his way.' she replied, holding his gaze.

'Our patience is not to be tested.' he continued, closing his jacket once again.

'It is quite ironic that you chose to meet here Miss Silankis.' said the eldest of the suited men. He, unlike the others, showed the slightest of emotions through a half smile. However, it was more sinister and mischievous than welcoming.

'We are stood on the birthplace of the persecution of Pagans in Roman occupied Brittania. This very site was once the Grand Forum of Colchester where the generals received their orders to eradicate the Pagans of this barbaric island.' He walked around the bandstand as he spoke. 'Before the Romans built Colchester, a more ancient site was erected here by Neolithic celts. This was the ritualistic site of barbarity and evil.'
'The Trinovantes sacrificial plinth.' answered Genevieve knowingly. 'I have heard all about how the invading forces discovered thousands of deviant burials surrounding a series of standing stones.'
The older man stared at her in silence. His pale eyes made her skin crawl.

'This is where the Romans built a huge monument to Camulos, the God of War. The Camulodunum Forum stood just there, at the very centre of the Roman settlement.' continued the smiling suit. Pointing up to the brow of the mound to the Norman castle that now stood there. 'They wanted to ensure that the locals couldn't continue their dark sacreligious practices. They tore down the stone monoliths and killed every person within a ten mile radius. The stamp of authority. The symbol of dominance. The sign of a new regime.'

'They were the barbarians.' retorted Genevieve in defiance. 'The Romans, and then the chauvinist Church that followed.'

The suited men glared at her audacity. One stepped forward grabbing her by the arms shaking her.

'How dare you speak to him like that, you filthy-' he erupted.

'Enough!' ordered the smiling suit, 'All will be revealed, let her go.' he ordered calmly as the other man released Genevieve without protest.

'What gives you the inclination of your comment Miss Silankis?' he asked openly.

'History is always written by the victor, the biassed opinion of those in control.' she started. 'The old religions scared the Romans, and later the Church. A religion led by and devoted to women. One that honoured and respected the beauty in the life making wonder that is human reproduction. But there was no barbarity in their practice, just simple equilibrium.' she frowned as she spoke, her voice strong and defiant. 'Misunderstanding, ignorance and fear has led to millions of deaths for thousands of years.'

'What are you talking about *woman*?' spat one of the suited men, his entire presence was that of annoyance and irritability. 'Where did you hear such stupid things?'

Genevieve raised her hands, shaking the Samsonite case and Capsa.

'You have read the blasphemous scriptures then.' said smiling suit rhetorically, he paced around the bandstand once again rubbing his face with his hands before placing them on his mouth.

'There is only truth within these cases.' she replied confidently.

The elder man checked his watch then looked around the park, 'Time is running out.' He nodded to his accomplice. Who stepped in towards Genevieve.

'Give me what is ours, and we will tell you the truth.' snapped one of the men irritably. He reached forward for the case and the Capsa.

'Release Sally and you can have them.' She pulled them away, taking a step backward.

'Let's compromise.' said another suited man tapping his watch impatiently.

'You broke the deal, Cortez is not here and your time is up Miss Silankis. Shoot her and DI Thorgood and bring me the documents.' Said suit one coldly.
The man standing closest to them pulled out his pistol from his suit jacket before training it on Sally's head.
A gunshot echoed throughout the parkland and everyone began screaming in terror as people fled to the exits across the parkland. Genevieve saw the muzzle flash from up in the tower of the castle above the grass bank. Her eyes focused on the small open tower window, she couldn't believe her eyes.

*

Massimo laughed as Cortez's eyes began to water. 'Paralysis is the worst, not being able to defend yourself. Only your eyes continue to work before all goes black.'

'Gum boots.' spat Cortez through gritted teeth. The Italian looked at him with a perplexed expression. Cortez headbutted the Italian on his already broken nose, sending him back several paces as his eyes rolled up.

'Ma come?' he spat irritably through a mouthful of fresh blood, his head spinning as nausea took over him. 'How did you-' Then he saw, he had missed them, what a foolish thing to not have seen. He fell to one knee as he nearly blacked out.

Cortez rubbed his neck and stood tall, spitting on the ground. 'Gum boots, or PowerMax RF800s to be precise. Certified to withstand 18kV.' Massimo looked outraged; his eyes wildly furious. Cortez stepped forward, now it was his turn to smile. 'Of course I have heard of Faraday you twit.' He looked up at the large white plastic cable running up the wall beside him, it ran from floor to ceiling, up to the radio transmission tower built into the roof and up into the large aerial that was erected at the top of the tower. Cortez grabbed the partially stunned Italian, releasing multiple devastating punches to his head, face and abdomen. Throwing him hard against the wall he pulled the plastic cabling away from the wall and wrapped it tightly around the dazed Massimo's torso and neck. 'I wrote a thesis on Faraday,' said Cortez, punching him once more. 'For my second Masters degree. One of the problems with Faraday's design is RF waves.' He sliced the aerial cabling's protective plastic casing open with his pocket knife in several places exposing the wires beneath and stood back. 'Exposure to high levels of RF waves result in the heating of the body temperature which the biological tissue can't cope with or release. Resulting in the skin cooking itself.'

Massimo grappled with the exposed cabling that now encircled his neck and torso, pinning him to the wall, trying with all his might to wriggle free. Cortez stepped forward once again.

'As for those sexy gloves,' he looked Massimo in the eye. 'Clever idea, but unfortunately it's a thumbs down from me.' he said pithily, grabbing both of Massimo's thumbs, ripping them down with two sickening cracks. Breaking both and tearing the tendons. 'Good luck untying yourself now you pompous prick.'

Massimo's face reddened as vapour began to emit from his shirt collar, he began to sweat profusely as his modified bespoke suit now acted as tin foil on a corn cob cooking him from within. He clawed helplessly at the cabling with his blood covered fingers, but without his thumbs it was useless. Cortez ran back to the window and raised the rifle, looking through the enhanced scope to see Sally standing with Genevieve and three men in dark suits. One of them pulled out a gun. "Genny!" he thought. He didn't hesitate.

"BANG"

As Cortez released the rifle trigger, he nodded to Genevieve who was staring directly up at him. The suited man dropped his gun, with his hand still attached to the grip as it fell to the ground silently. Cortez had blown the suited man's hand off at the wrist.

Cortez released three more successive shots into the roof of the bandstand causing a crescendo of three loud thuds and scattering splinters everywhere as the once tranquil landscape garden erupted into utter chaos as the families, couples, day trippers and dog walkers frantically ran for their lives.

'Down!' shouted suit one as the older suited man dropped to the wooden floor of the bandstand taking cover. The stunned man looked down at where his hand used to be, at the stub that now squirted warm blood all over his face and neck.

The two ladies exchanged a look and nodded. Genevieve swung the Samsonite case at the crouching old man's head as Sally drop kicked the other in the groin sending them both to the deck.
'After them, you idiot!' shouted the older suit. 'They must not escape.' The second suit stood to go after them but the roof exploded as Cortez released another shot from the high powered rifle. 'Call for backup!' he screamed as he aided the one who had just lost his left hand. Using his crossed-key handkerchief to stem the blood that now spurted over both their faces.

Penny and Elizabeth emerged from the nearest tree, cameras in hand. 'This way!' they shouted in unison as they ran back to the castle up the steep grass bank.
Genevieve and Sally needed no encouragement as they sprinted up after them.

They sprinted off back towards the castle walkway entrance as Cortez covered them from his vantage point directly above. Once he could see that both Sally and Genevieve were out of sight and inside he wiped down the rifle with his t-shirt and turned to Massimo who was still smoking in the corner.

'You don't deserve this, but I can't leave you to die like this.' said Cortez bluntly. 'I'm done taking lives, besides,' he exhaled loudly, 'I don't want your face haunting my dreams.' Massimo looked at him, unable to decipher what was going on. Was this weakness, or cowardice?

'They haunt your dreams too?' asked the Italian openly. His mind raced back to the face of Sister Margarette and the hundreds he had killed.

Cortez eyed the man bound to the wall. Something had changed in the Italians' dark eyes.

'But,' started Cortez, holding up his finger, choosing to ignore the man's question, 'If I see you again, I will not be so hospitable.'

Massimo nodded in acceptance, the last thing he saw was Cortez's large fist hurling towards his face before all went dark.

*

Sally removed the clear tape from her mouth and cursed strongly. 'Where the fuck is Cortez?' she shouted at Genevieve as they charged along the wooden gangplank up to the castle gate entrance.

'I don't know, he was supposed to meet me at the bandstand.' she replied breathlessly.

Penny and Elizabeth appeared from the right grated doorway ahead of them ashen faced and panting.

They both ushered them forward and into the castle entrance, then Penny screamed,

'Behind you! Look out!' she pointed at the trees behind them directly opposite the entrance as three more suited men appeared from different directions, closing in on them.

'Quickly, down to the undercroft.' spat Elizabeth, running off to the right towards the large well opening in the centre of the room. Off to the left of this room she pulled open the iron grated door that read, "S.C.". Behind the door stood a staircase that led down into darkness. Outside they could hear the three men's feet pounding along the wooden ramp, each step getting ever closer.

They took several steps at a time, more jumping than stepping until they reached the vaulted stone chamber traditionally used as the cellar and dungeon before the prison was moved to the ground floor.

Originally this vast space was used to store barrels, crates, prisoners and weaponry. It was now used to store the castle's touristic elements, dozens of boxes of brochures, posters, cleaning equipment, brooms, mops, wooden toys and old displays filled the space beneath the popular attraction. Off to the side stood an impressive looking ballista.

The dim lighting made it difficult to see to the end of the chamber, 'Is there another way out?' called Sally as she looked back up the staircase.

'These are the Roman sections of the castle. The original walls of the Temple of Claudius and the Forum.' continued Elizabeth, pointing to the red brick and carved stone blocks on each of the pillars, arches and walls. 'It loops around but there is supposedly a hidden passage that leads through the back.'

'Supposedly?' questioned Sally aghast. 'You mean we could have made ourselves sitting ducks?'

Shadows of the three suited men appeared on the wall above them. She placed a finger on her lips to silence the other ladies as she pushed them deeper into the glim basement cavern beneath the castle.

The men spoke with a European accent as they descended the steps, Genevieve recognised it as Swiss. The three suits entered the room and began searching for their prey. The ladies moved back slowly and silently, embarking on a game of hide and seek amongst the boxes and crates.

Along each of the arches beneath the ancient colonnade stood ornate old iron grated gates and bricked up walls that partitioned off areas. One of the grated gates opened into a smaller antechamber with four windowed cell doors along two of the side walls. In the centre of the room was a hatch that led into a deep pit.

'Is this an oubliette?' asked Genevieve looking down into the darkness. 'I have an idea.' she smiled.
The three men rounded the corner to find the grated door open. They stepped cautiously inside as they took a cell door each to inspect the contents.
'C'est vide.' said one with a heavy sigh. 'It is empty.'
'Yes, they are all empty.' replied another looking at the two empty cells on his side of the room.
The third man held up his hand, his eyes focused on the hatch in the centre of the room. He pointed down to it and sneered tapping his ear.
Below in the darkness they could hear four female voices whispering.
'Grüezi,' spoke one of the suits, down into the darkness. The voices stopped.
'Come out, don't make this harder than it has to be.' called another suit.

They were met with silence, then more whispering. It wasn't long before they received a reply.
'We are stuck, it's too deep, you will have to climb down and help us out,' said Genevieve from the darkness.
'Throw up the case and the Capsa, and we will let you live,' called one of the suits.
'You would leave us to die down here. We are not stupid.' replied Elizabeth indignantly.

'Oh but you are, ALL WOMEN ARE.' sneered the suit bitterly, as the three men laughed and looked down into the darkness. The visibility was so poor that they could only see several feet down. One pointed to the other, 'I volunteer you to climb down,' he said confidently, obviously the leader. 'We will wait here and pull you and the women back up.'

'Why not use some rope?' he protested, raising his arms.

'You see any rope?' snapped the leader in retort, looking around the old cells.

The suit rolled his eyes but did as he was told.

'If you try anything funny, we will shoot.' shouted the leader deep into the darkness.

They lowered their friend down by his arms until he was out of sight.

It was then that they heard the thud from behind them.

Spinning on the spot the first man ducked as a long thin projectile with a bristled end came hurtling towards his face. It hit his colleague standing directly behind him square in the face sending him backwards and to the ground, hard and fast. The first man glanced back at his incapacitated friend and the broom that lay on top of his unconscious body. He snapped back to the doorway where he had to double take at what he was seeing. To his confused astonishment he was looking at a Roman ballista, just as two ladies were placing a mop onto its upper track. At the same time another two ladies had been winding the two handles back, arming it.

'What the fu-' started the suit as the mop head and pole hurtled towards him at 300 feet per second. He didn't manage to duck this one. The impact into his chest was sickening, the felt strands of the mop head had no cushioning effect at this speed. The wooden shaft and metal mount that attaches the mop to its handle were as effective as an ancient Roman ballista bolt.

From deep in the abyss of the oubliette suit number three called up, 'Scheisse! There is just a mobile phone down here. Looks like they have fooled us,' he shouted again. 'Guys? What is going on up there?'

Genevieve and Sally pulled the grated door shut and slid the door bolt across. A look of pure satisfaction on their faces. 'Who is stupid?' They called through the bars. *'Who runs the world?'* They sang together in chorus, *'Girls!'*

'Just like Boudica did in 60 AD, leave it to the women to get the job done and take care of the chauvinist pigs in Colchester.' smiled Elizabeth.
'Work smart, not hard,' laughed Penny, disconnecting their group call on her phone. They ran back along the tunnels to the base of the staircase. 'Would it be too clichéd to say *"Girl Power"* at this point?'
'Too late,' laughed Elizabeth in reply.

'Wait,' hissed Sally, taking Penny's arm, sending them back around the corner out of sight, 'There is another one coming down.' she pushed herself against the wall, ready to pounce. The large figure bounded down the steps at breakneck speed, Sally unleashed a powerful kick to the large man's midriff as he reached the bottom step.
'Bloody hell Sally!' shouted Cortez as he doubled over.
'Och Hen,' she started apologetically, helping her old friend up. 'I thought you were another one of the *Ordo Solis.'*
Cortez just glared at her for a moment, he looked down at his torn and bloodied AC/DC t-shirt and gold chains then back up to meet Sally's face now showing regret. He shook his head then released a gentle smile as Penny, Genevieve and Elizabeth emerged back into the light from above the staircase. 'Genny!' he called, stepping across to embrace her. 'You ok Dove?'

She pushed him back looking at his battered face, 'Never mind me, what happened to you?' She touched his blood encrusted face and beard. Welts and bruises swelling, contorting his already rough features.

'Jesus Cortez!' called Sally, 'You been opening doors with your face or somethin'? You look bloody terrible.'

'The Italian, Massimo,' started Cortez, pointing behind him with his thumb. Before he lowered it awkwardly.

'Let's get the fuck out o' here!' shouted Sally running up the stairs back into the ground floor of the castle. Cortez went out first to check for any more *Ordo Solis* soldiers. They ran together through the deserted park, then Cortez dipped off through some bushes, waving them to carry on without him. They only heard a crunching sound as the foliage rustled.

It took two minutes to reach Ryegate Road, the four ladies arrived back at Beth the lab technician's car. Genevieve looked across to them looking at their hands for their phones. 'Did you get it?' she asked, her voice distraught. 'At the bandstand?'

'We got everything,' smiled Penny, opening the rear passenger door. 'Come on, we have to move.'

Sally was pushed up against the car window by an invisible force as her face contorted and she cried out in agony. The three ladies looked back up the road to see another suited man with a pistol raised.

'How many of these arse holes are there?' screamed Elizabeth pulling open the car door.

'Get in the sodding car you idiots!' shouted Sally clambering into the back seat lying on her front. Elizabeth jumped in after her, taking off her shirt to dress the wound in Sally's elbow as she applied pressure to the red stain. 'Why the fuck are we no' driving away?' shouted Sally.

Genevieve looked back at them in shock. 'Cortez has the keys.'

The near side windows burst inwards as two more shots were fired by the approaching suit man. The four ladies screamed as they ducked down below the car door, seeking cover where there was none to be found.

The armed man walked confidently closer as he called to them to throw the case and Capsa outside the vehicle. Now only five feet away he shouted again. 'Throw out the documents and I will not kill you.'

From their crouched position they could only hear the man outside. Not being able to see him, the next few sounds were not expected. Tyres screeched nearby followed by a thud then their car moved sideways by two feet sending them across to the other side of the vehicle with a painful jolt. Genevieve looked up to see the suited man now pressed against where the windows used to be. He had been run over and forced forward by the impact, only to be pinned by the electric Range Rover that had T-boned them and was now directly beside them. Genevieve looked through the windscreen of the Range Rover to see Nicola Stirling's gloved hands on the steering wheel. Her two daughters sat in the passenger and rear passenger seat. What was more confusing was that the rear passenger seat directly behind Nicola was occupied by none other than Flint.

Cortez rounded the corner out of the parkland to the scene that had just played out. He frowned but shook his head and ran over to the car pulling off the either dead or unconscious suited man laying him on the ground. He pocketed the dropped pistol and opened the driver's door. Pulling Genevieve out he kissed her strongly and squeezed her so tightly that she had to tap his shoulders to ease up.

'Och, now he turns up.' shouted Sally angrily. 'You're late to the party,' she whined. 'Where are the keys?'

'Late?' he repeated mockingly. He half contemplated using the famous Gandalf quote about never being late and arriving precisely when he intended to, but he quickly thought the better of it when he saw her bloodied arm. 'I am so sorry,' he started, 'These *Ordo Solis* are like cockroaches.' he said pointing back over his shoulder.
'Oh, your face.' remarked Genevieve as she again patted Cortez's pummelled face.

'As sweet as this is!' shouted Sally sarcastically from the back seat, 'Can we get the fuck on?!' She pulled herself up and continued to shout at her friend. 'In case you may have forgotten, there are most likely more of those fuckers in the park if not more about to come around that corner in armoured vehicles and in case it escaped you, I have been shot,' she lifted her bleeding arm up to show Cortez.

'I'll drive,' he said. 'Follow us. We're taking Sally to the hospital.' he called through the window of Nicola's car.
'Beth is not going to be happy with what you did to her car.' he half joked as they pulled away. The side was completely indented, buckled and both windows were missing, let alone the blood spatters along one side.

Cortez took his phone out of his thigh pocket to see the screen had been cracked, in the centre of the crack was the shape of a knife point. The Italians knife blade. He blew out his cheeks at the realisation that had he not had his phone in there he probably would have bled out from the near femoral artery injury. He tossed the dead phone into the footwell and asked Genevieve for her phone.

'Police Officer DI Thorgood has been shot, left humerus, minor bleed.' said Cortez into the handset.
'Minor, you cheeky bastard!' she shouted from the back. 'It hurts like hell.'

'Yes, that was her, conscious, breathing and shouting. Notify the trauma unit at Colchester Hospital, ETA is seven minutes.' he rang off and passed the phone back to Genevieve. 'You got a missed call.' he said absently as he drove.

'Are you not going to tell the police about what happened?' asked Penny agog.

'Do you not think that the twenty gunshots and dozens of the members of the public running and screaming for their lives will be enough for them to know that something has happened?' asked Sally plainly, her dry sense of humour lost on Penny.

As she said this, as if on cue police sirens filled the air from every direction.

'First we sort you out Sally, then we figure out what step two is.' he slowed as he came to the end of Ryegate Road, the front of the castle and the Claudius Temple ruin lay just beside them. He looked down to the Capsa between Genevieve's legs.

'You think he wrote that in there?' he asked aloud. He could not help but envisage that two thousand years before, Emperor Claudius may have sat in that very building lit by oil lamps and glowing braziers to write the scroll detailing his secret journey across Britannia in which he had learnt the sacred knowledge of the ancient Pagan ritualistic procession along one hundred and eleven Neolithic standing stones running from what would later become known as Winchester to the site of Colchester.

He was half tempted to stop the car and walk it back to the ruin to lay it upon the stones. To feel the buzz that he felt on returning ancient relics to their former haunts, origins or inceptions.

He slammed on the brakes as someone jumped in front of their car. 'You have got to be kidding me!' he spat as the battered, dishevelled and heavily bruised Massimo limped in front of them blocking their exit along Museum Street onto the High Street.

'Just run him over!' shouted Sally. 'What?' she asked as the others turned to look at her.

Cortez locked eyes on the hitman, 'So you have chosen death…' he mouthed quietly.

The car door took some force to open following the impact from the Range Rover but he climbed out and walked to the front of the vehicle. 'You not remember what I said?'

Massimo looked between Cortez and Genevieve then to the others in the back of the car. Then to the Stirlings in the vehicle behind. 'You have something that I want.' he started.

'Look, it's over. Walk away.' shouted Cortez. 'You are not getting the scroll or the Wren documents.'

Massimo laughed, 'It is not these that I want. It is this…' he said pointing his mangled hands to the people in the vehicles. 'The love, the friendship… the loyalty.' he sighed.

Cortez turned to look at his friends within the vehicle. 'Last chance, walk away.'

Massimo closed his eyes. Then nodded as he limped away. 'You will need this,' he shouted, throwing a small USB stick to Cortez. 'It has every telephone call, email and financial transaction made by the *Ordo Solis* to orchestrate yours and a dozen other deaths.'

Cortez pocketed the USB and turned to walk away, but he could not fight the temptation of curiosity, so he turned back to the Italian. 'Why are you now helping us?'

'Morto che cammina… I am a dead man walking. So why not?' he laughed.

'If I had wanted you dead, you would have died back in Westminster Abbey. I had followed you both for ten minutes before I made myself known to you.' he half smiled, half winced in pain.

'Eight times since I have had you both in my sights, but I did not fire.' He stepped forward again. 'Your quest is a noble one. That is why I killed Major Calvin Montgomery and Armon Di Silva.' he looked down to his rent and deformed hands. 'I wanted to give you a hand.' he laughed heartily, coughing through dried blood from his nose.

'Calvin was one of the good guys, Massimo.' called Cortez solemnly.

The Italian shook his head, 'No, he was dirty. He had been selling The Royal Society secrets to the *Ordo Solis* for years. He was about to hand over the Wren documents. Your friend,' he pointed his broken hand to Penny, 'She asked too many questions. Raised too many eyebrows that would cause trouble for Montgomery. She was on my list, so was Cappuccetto Rosso.' he again pointed to the vehicle's occupants, this time Elizabeth.

Cortez looked back to Penny and Elizabeth. 'Why would they want to kill them?' he asked openly. 'Before today they were not involved?'

'Oh but they were.' answered the Italian, 'For months now cogs have been turning in the background. Leading to this moment.'

Sirens now blasted from all around them. The emergency response vehicles were no more than one minute out.

'Next thing you're going to tell me is that Flint was involved too.' said Cortez.

'Who is Flint?' replied Massimo, a puzzled look on his face.

'What, you're telling me of all those involved in this you don't know a man like Flint?'

Massimo just shrugged his shoulders in response.

'He is sitting just there, in the Range Rover.' laughed Cortez. A car door opened behind him, causing Cortez to turn on his heel. 'Speak of the devil.' quipped Cortez. 'Say his name and he appears.'

Massimo looked at the man approaching them. His eyes squinted in to focus better on the man's face. He never forgot a face, and he recognised this man instantly. 'His name is not Flint!' he shouted. 'He is Lord Stirling, the benefactor for-'

"BANG"

Cortez spun again to see Flint holding a Beretta 92F 9mm cradled in his hands. Looking back he saw Massimo now spread-eagled prone on the floor.

'Whatever he just gave you, hand it over.' snapped Flint in trepidation. 'Come on, empty your pockets.'

'What is going on here, Flint?' challenged Cortez. He watched as Nicola removed the Samsonite case and Capsa from Genevieve's lap as Anne held a gun over them.

'Nullius in verba' spat Flint. 'Take nobody's word for it.'

'The police will be here any second Flint.' shouted Cortez as the deafening sirens wailed all around them.

'More incentive for you to hand over whatever it was he just gave you.' Flint looked panicked, his face was pale and he was sweating profusely. 'Don't make me kill you Cortez.'

'He called you Stirling.' said Cortez loudly. 'As in the late Lord Stirling, who died in a skiing accident a decade ago?'

'Be quiet!' he shouted in protest. 'I *will* shoot you.' he shook the Beretta at Cortez menacingly.

'You son of a bitch. You played us all along, sInce Cambridge.' spat Cortez growing more and more despondent.

'You have no idea what I have had to sacrifice. How much I have had to lose to orchestrate all of this. Our family has been through years of trouble because of the Church. The Ordo Solis betrayed my family, took our land, our money and left us with huge debts.' Flint walked closer to Cortez, his eyes red and wild. 'Those animals tortured my wife, they made her hold a silver crucifix as they poured boiling water over her hands.' He turned to look back at Nicola and then down to her gloved hands. 'I want to take back what we are owed!'

'So this is all about revenge?' started Cortez. Blue lights now flickered off taller buildings just streets away.

'Right, enough, hands on your head, I will get it myself.' he said leaning in closer to Cortez putting his hand inside Cortez's pocket. 'Where is it?' he snapped.

'Father, come on!' shouted Catherine from the Range Rover. Flint grabbed something out of Cortez's pocket and ran back to meet his family before they sped off back along Ryegate Road as two ARVs armed response vehicles swung around from the High Street.

Cortez laid down placing the pistol he had taken from the dead suit man beside him and placed his hands on his head. He had been trained how to act in this situation and he knew compliance was always the right way.

But to his astonishment the ARV units just sped off past him chasing the electric Range Rover up the one-way street.

Sally poked her head out of the window, 'Been on the blower the entire time. They heard everything.' she winced as she accidentally leant on her injured elbow. 'Can you please get me to the bloody hospital now!'

Cortez stood up, placing the gun back in his belt as he walked back to the car. Climbing into the driver's seat he looked back across the road where Massimo had been laying on his back. Only to find that he had disappeared in all the commotion. 'Kevlar suit.' he muttered to himself as he started the engine. 'I'd like to meet his tailor.'

The end of the High Street has been cordoned off by regular police units, but one flash from DI Thorgood's badge entitled them to a well deserved police escort to Colchester Hospital.

*

Once Sally had received treatment for her injuries she was sat up in the hospital gurney in a private room with all of the others sitting around her.

'I got you something.' smiled Cortez. Handing her a long gift bag. He too had received some attention to all the cuts and bruises that adorned his furry face.
'It better be scotch.' she laughed as she opened it. 'Oh you fucking beauty,' she laughed even harder as she pulled out a bottle of Irn-Bru.

'So,' she huffed loudly. 'That was not what I was expecting when I offered to help you's out.' she smiled at her old friend. 'So they got away with all of the evidence, and the hitman's USB.' She folded her arms and shook her head.

'Actually,' interrupted Genevieve, 'They got away with the Samsonite case and the Capsa, but they were both empty. I opened them both whilst Cortez was talking to Massimo. I put them in the glove box and under the seat. Women's intuition.' She pulled them out of her bag and laid them on the bed.

'As for the USB stick.' laughed Cortez, putting his hand into his pocket. He pulled it out and placed it on the wheelie table in front of Sally. 'The bugger only went and took my lucky pocket knife.'

Sally looked at the documents and the USB, then up to all of them stood around her. 'Right then, somebody get me a pen and some paper for all your statements and a glass for my Irn-Bru.' she laughed. 'This is going to be a long fucking night.'

*

Unknown Location
Rome

The birthmarked Cardinal fell to the floor heavily, his crimson red robes fanned out around him. He muttered something under his breath and attempted to turn onto his back.
A stylish young woman stood above him, her hands holding a silenced Sig Sauer pistol.
'Sacrilegio…' he gasped. 'Come osi!'
'Send a woman to do a man's job.' she called as the Cardinal crawled away on his elbows.

'Hai il coraggio di essere in questa stanza sacra.' The man muttered desperately as he fled. 'You dare to enter this sacred room?' His robe hindered him as he became more and more entangled within it.

'Welcome to the new world.' she lowered her pistol, training it on the rear of his crimson cap.

"Thut thut thut thut"

The young woman turned away, taking out her mobile phone. She messaged her handler and within seconds a message appeared stating she had received €100,000 into her bank account,

Even in the contract killing business there was a discriminatory gender pay gap.

New Message:
<Target: Massimo Lupo, Alias: The Wolf, EXTREMELY DANGEROUS, €3,000,000>

'Now this is a job that will get me noticed.' She placed her pistol into her holster and called her handler directly. 'Where was he last seen?'

*

Genevieve's Apartment, London

The following day multiple newsreels had been broadcasting images of the Stirling family and the until now, believed to be dead, Mr Stirling, in association with the multiple shootings that had transpired across England over the last week. Details of an ancient conspiracy and church cover up had started to rumble and soon grew to a massive story on all channels and stations as more and more publications and evidence was released following the investigation by DI Thorgood.

Genevieve and Cortez sat in her flat watching the latest updates on the evening news on the developing saga when the news anchor announced that the Catholic Church *"still refused to comment"* on the subject but they were going live to DI Thorgood for an important announcement.

"The man fraudulently claiming to be Flint was in fact Lord Stirling who had faked his own death a decade ago to escape public attention. This man had subsequently spent the last decade using his family wealth to orchestrate and manufacture multiple murders and false information to further his goal of disclosing the hidden knowledge of the path-way that historically ran through his ancestral home. It has not yet become clear as to why he had taken these actions but I am certain that as we further our investigations we will uncover more secrets and hopefully the plot behind his clandestine venture."

A reporter was then heard off camera asking about how Flint had been using people.

"Flint had indeed been using multiple people for information gathering, mostly though the deception was unbeknownst to them. Imagine a puppet master holding dozens of invisible strings. We are still unravelling the enormous web of deceit and lies that has been spun by this man and his family."

Another reporter off camera asked if The Royal Society had been in cahoots with Lord Stirling.

"No. Flint is not associated with the Royal Society, far from it. Any such publications that state that he is or was, will be discredited and liable for prosecution." Several groans were heard from the journalists off camera.

"Flint, or rather Lord Stirling, knew that the older members of the Royal Society would recognize him. That is why he couldn't return there and this was why he approached younger members of staff to continue his work. It also transpires that the recent murder of Major Montgomery was also linked to the Stirling Family."

Many reporters were heard shouting questions all relating to the Catholic Church and their association with the Crossed Keys, the ancient Order of the Sun or *Ordo Solis*.

"At this time all questions associated with the Catholic Church have been going through the respective legal teams and as such I am not at liberty to say anything. Thank you, that is all for now."

It switched back to the news anchor who made some quip about religion before going over to the sports report.

'Fancy a cuppa Genny?' asked Cortez as he stood up with a stretch. She nodded and pulled him down to kiss his large fuzzy face.
He walked through to the dark kitchen and flicked the wall switch. 'You not fixed this bulb yet Dove?'
'Oh no, sorry, I keep forgetting about it,' she replied apologetically. 'I'll buy one tomorrow I promise.'

He huffed indignantly but continued to turn on the kettle, the appliance's transparent glass turning a blue colour as it began to boil. He opened the fridge to remove the milk then paused. His eyes caught a glimpse of something familiar on the dining table in the centre of the room. Something that should not have been there. His old lucky pocket knife.

Spinning quickly he grabbed a large kitchen knife from the sideboard and raised it above his head ready to strike.

The turbulent blue light effervesced around the room as a small silhouette moved in the corner of the room.

'Genevieve!' he shouted through to the other room but was met with only silence.
A strobed torch beam blinked on and off blinding his eyes as he swung forward, he tried to move through to the lounge but he was struck from behind by a second silhouette as all went black.

*

To be continued.

Printed in Great Britain
by Amazon